A FRIEND IN NEED

Lisa wasted no time before heading for Pepper's stall. She didn't even stop to greet the curious horses who looked out and nickered as she passed, though she supposed they were probably wondering what she was doing there at this hour.

Lisa had almost grown accustomed to not seeing Pepper's head poking out to greet her as she approached, since these days he seemed to spend most of his time with his head hanging low, facing the back of the stall. She wouldn't have been surprised to see that. But she was surprised by what she did see when she opened the stall door. Pepper was lying on his side in the straw, breathing hard.

THE SADDLE CLUB

AUTUMN TRAIL

BONNIE BRYANT

A BANTAM SKYLARK BOOK®
NEW YORK • TORONTO • LONDON • SYDNEY • AUCKLAND

RL 5, 009–012

AUTUMN TRAIL

A Bantam Skylark Book / October 1993

Skylark Books is a registered trademark of Bantam Books,
a division of Bantam Doubleday Dell Publishing Group, Inc.
Registered in U.S. Patent and Trademark Office and elsewhere.

"The Saddle Club" is a trademark of Bonnie Bryant Hiller.
The Saddle Club design / logo, which consists of an inverted
U-shaped design, a riding crop, and a riding hat is a
trademark of Bantam Books.

ISBN 0-553-48077-4

Published simultaneously in the United States and Canada

Bantam Books are published by Bantam Books, a division of Bantam
Doubleday Dell Publishing Group, Inc. Its trademark, consisting of the
words "Bantam Books" and the portrayal of a rooster, is Registered in
U.S. Patent and Trademark Office and in other countries. Marca Regis-
trada. Bantam Books, 1540 Broadway, New York, New York 10036.

PRINTED IN THE UNITED STATES OF AMERICA

OPM   0 9 8 7 6 5 4 3 2 1

I would like to express my special thanks to Catherine Hapka for her help in the writing of this book.

1

"I CAN'T BELIEVE I'm saying this," Carole Hanson said through chattering teeth, "but I'm glad this ride is almost over."

Carole's two best friends, Stevie Lake and Lisa Atwood, looked at her in amazement. "*I* can't believe you're saying it, either," Stevie teased. "You mean you're actually *tired* of riding?"

Stevie knew very well that if there was one thing Carole never tired of, it was riding. In fact, Carole, Stevie, and Lisa all loved riding—and everything else about horses—so much that they had formed a group called The Saddle Club. It had only two rules. The first was that members had to be horse crazy, and the second was that they always had to be willing to help one another out with any problem, large or small.

"Very funny. I mean I'm freezing to death," Carole responded. She tried to glare at Stevie, but found that a bit difficult, since her eyebrows were frozen in place. She soon gave up and laughed instead. "I guess this will teach me to listen to the weather report more often. Maybe the next time it's this cold, I'll know to wear a warmer coat."

The three girls were riding on one of the trails that wound through the woods behind Pine Hollow Stables, where they all took riding lessons and where Carole boarded her horse, Starlight. The weather was unusually cold for mid-November in northern Virginia. The night before, the temperature had dropped below freezing. Today, even though it was only late afternoon, it was already bitterly cold.

"I'm wearing the warmest coat I have, and I'm frozen, too," Lisa said. "I can't believe it's this cold and it's not even Thanksgiving yet. At this rate it'll be forty below zero by January." She gave an involuntary shiver at the thought.

"It feels like it's forty below *now*," Carole declared. Starlight snorted as if in agreement, sending a puff of steam into the frosty air. "See? Even Starlight thinks it's too cold to be out here."

"No, that's not what he said," Stevie corrected with a mischievous grin. "He thinks you're just being selfish. After all, he needs his exercise, no matter what the weather's like."

"I know," Carole said, giving the horse a pat on the neck. "Sorry, Starlight." Carole took her responsibilities as a horse owner very seriously. The beautiful bay gelding had been a surprise Christmas present from her father the year before.

A few seconds later Carole realized that Stevie had been teasing her again. "How do you know what Starlight was saying, anyway? You know how Max is always saying that horses don't understand English. I bet he'd have a hard time believing you understand Horse."

Max was the owner of Pine Hollow and the girls' riding instructor. He was constantly teaching his riders not to tell their horses what to do in words. Even though some horses seemed to understand a few words, and the tone of a rider's voice often conveyed meaning to his or her mount, Carole knew that the best way for riders to get their horses to do what they wanted was with their hands, legs, and seat.

Stevie knew it, too, but at this particular moment she decided to ignore Carole's teasing and continue her previous thought. "Still," she said, "I don't think Starlight would object if we trotted for a while. We can move back down to a walk when we get to the meadow."

"Great idea," Carole said enthusiastically. "That way the horses will get their exercise, and we'll get back to the stable faster."

"And we can post to keep warm," Lisa added.

3

"Exactly what I was thinking," Stevie said. "Come on, let's go."

The girls signaled for their horses to trot. By this time they were on the smooth, well-worn section of the trail leading to the wide meadow that separated the woods from the pastures behind Pine Hollow. As they left the woods a few minutes later, the girls slowed their horses back down to a walk. It was important for the horses to have a chance to cool down after their exercise before being put back in their stalls, and no matter how cold they were, the girls wouldn't even consider breaking this rule.

As they moved across the meadow, Lisa's eye moved automatically to the pasture where Pepper lived. Pepper had been a Pine Hollow institution for years. He was the horse that Max had usually assigned to new riders, for he was gentle and patient and had a way of teaching them —sometimes even better than Max could, although none of the girls would ever have wanted to be the one to tell Max that! Lisa hadn't been riding as long as Carole and Stevie had; in fact, Pepper was one of the first horses she had ever ridden, and he had been her favorite mount until his recent retirement.

It had been difficult for Lisa to accept the fact that Pepper was just too old to be ridden anymore, but she had finally realized that the faithful horse deserved a rest. Stevie had even arranged a retirement party for him, so that all the riders who had learned from Pepper over the years could come and thank him. Now Pepper spent his days peacefully grazing in the shady pasture the girls were passing.

At this moment, though, Lisa thought that Pepper's pasture looked anything but inviting. The sun was just setting, and its last rays sent harsh shadows across the grayish, frostbitten grass. Lisa could just make out the shape of Pepper, covered in a warm wool stable blanket. He was standing near the fence on the opposite side of the pasture, closest to the stable. His head was hanging low, and he seemed to be staring in the direction of the buildings.

"Look, you guys," Lisa said, interrupting Carole and Stevie, who were still trading joking insults. At the worried tone in her voice, both of them turned immediately to see what was wrong. Lisa pointed at the still form of the old gray horse. "Do you think it's too cold for Pepper to be out here all night?"

Carole nodded, looking concerned. "Definitely. No horse should stay out too long in this kind of weather, especially not one as old as Pepper. I'm surprised Max hasn't brought him in already."

"I think I'll ask Max if we can bring him in for the night as soon as we get back," Lisa said. She gave a last glance at Pepper as she rode on after the others. She noticed that he didn't even look around as the girls rode past his pasture. That wasn't like him. Normally he would have hurried over to the fence so that they would stop and visit with him for a while. Lisa wondered if she should mention it to the others. One of the first things she had learned at Pine Hollow was to watch the horses for odd or unusual behavior, since it was often an early warning sign of illness or injury.

Lisa glanced at Pepper again and decided to keep quiet. She was sure that in this case it was just the cold weather that was making Pepper act strange. But she promised herself she would check him over carefully when they brought him inside.

Her thoughts were interrupted as Stevie pulled her horse, Topside, up next to Lisa's mount, Barq. "Hey, Lisa, I hope you've got hot chocolate at your house," Stevie said. The three girls were going to the Atwoods' house for a sleepover after their ride. "Carole and I have decided we definitely have a craving."

Lisa smiled, trying to erase from her mind the image of Pepper standing motionless by the fence. "You bet we do."

A LITTLE OVER an hour later, the three girls were settled comfortably in Lisa's pink-and-white bedroom, steaming cups of hot cocoa in their hands. "This is more like it," Carole said with a sigh. "I was beginning to think I'd never be warm again." She snuggled down deeper into the overstuffed chair she was curled up in.

"I'll bet Pepper thought that, too," Lisa said. "He looked so grateful when we brought him inside."

"And Max says horses and people don't speak the same language," Stevie said with a sniff.

"I'm just glad Max said it was okay to bring Pepper inside," Lisa said. "In fact, he said he'd been planning to send Red out to bring him in anyway. He said this cold snap took him a little by surprise, and he wishes he'd brought Pepper in last night, too." She took a sip of cocoa, almost burning her tongue because she was so distracted thinking about Pepper. "I just hope he's all right."

"Me, too," Carole said. "By the way, speaking of Red, did you all happen to notice which horse he had just finished exercising when we came in?" Red O'Malley was the head stable hand at Pine Hollow.

Stevie nodded. "Who else? Garnet, of course."

Garnet was a spirited chestnut mare that belonged to Veronica diAngelo, a spoiled rich girl who rode at Pine Hollow and also went to the private school Stevie attended. The diAngelos were the wealthiest family in Willow Creek, and Veronica seemed to think that meant she could make everyone else do her chores and take care of her horse—especially Red, whom Veronica often seemed to regard as her own personal groom.

"I'd noticed that Veronica hadn't been around much lately," Stevie continued. "Red told me she hasn't been in to ride in almost a week. Poor Garnet was going crazy with boredom, even though Max has been letting her out in the paddock every day. So Red decided to take her out for a quick ride before she started trying to kick down her stall."

"That's terrible," Carole said, shaking her head in disgust. She had no patience for riders who didn't take proper care of their horses, and Veronica was definitely one of those. In fact, Veronica's carelessness had caused the death of the horse she'd owned before Garnet, a beautiful coal-black Thoroughbred stallion named Cobalt. Carole had loved and taken care of Cobalt more than Veronica had herself, and his death had almost made her want to give up riding forever. She had long since changed her mind about that, but the experience had made her even more critical of Veronica's lazy habits. "That girl should not be allowed anywhere near a stable. I don't know how she can be so selfish sometimes. She never thinks of anyone but herself, let alone her horse."

"Well, she'll have to show up soon," Lisa said. "I heard Max saying that she had to be there on Monday when the farrier comes to put new shoes on Garnet."

"I guess he's still hoping she'll learn something one of these days," Stevie said.

"I wouldn't count on it," Carole said. "She won't learn because she doesn't want to learn."

"Speaking of learning," Stevie said, "Monday is the day my school is putting on its famous stupid Thanksgiving play. Ugh. I thought they'd learned their lesson last year when the whole audience fell asleep."

8

Carole and Lisa laughed. They both went to the public school in Willow Creek. "Come on, Stevie," Carole said. "What's wrong with putting on a Thanksgiving play? I think it's a nice way to celebrate the holiday."

"You wouldn't say that if you'd ever seen it," Stevie said. "Believe me, it's totally corny. It doesn't have anything to do with the true meaning of Thanksgiving."

"What do you mean?" Lisa asked. "What's the play about?"

"Well, you know, the usual stuff," Stevie said, waving one hand and almost spilling her cocoa. "The Pilgrims sail across the ocean from England and land on Plymouth Rock, and the Native Americans meet them, and they all help each other out and grow some crops and then thank each other and sit down to eat. It's the same thing every year."

Carole shrugged. "That's the story of the first Thanksgiving."

"Right," Lisa said. "It sounds nice. Seeing the play probably reminds people to be thankful for what they have."

"Exactly," Stevie said with a nod. "People get caught up in the thankful part of it, and they forget all about helping people. That's part of Thanksgiving, too. Those Pilgrims were thankful because the Native Americans they met helped them to survive, even though they really didn't have to do it. They just did it because they were nice enough to want to help someone else out.

That's the part a lot of people don't really seem to care about celebrating, and it's the part that's always seemed the most important to me."

Carole and Lisa exchanged a perplexed glance. It wasn't like Stevie to get so worked up about something like this. She wasn't exactly the philosophical type.

"I just don't see anything wrong with putting on a Thanksgiving play," Carole insisted. "I think it's good to be thankful for what we have."

"I'm not saying putting on a play is a bad thing. Neither is being thankful," Stevie said. "But it just seems to me that there should be more to it than that. After all, there are plenty of people out there who have a lot less to be thankful for than we do."

Lisa nodded thoughtfully. "For instance, the descendants of the Native Americans, who've lost most of their land." Lisa was an excellent student, and she could always be counted on to point out the facts that the others sometimes forgot. Her class had been studying the history of Native Americans, and she had learned that one result of the Wampanoag tribe's helpfulness to the first European visitors to North America had been that more of those visitors soon followed. Eventually many Native Americans were killed by European diseases or by the Europeans themselves, and those who survived lost most of the land that they'd lived on for generations.

"That's true," Carole said. "I wonder what Christine would think about your play, Stevie?" Christine Lonetree was a Native American girl who was a member of the western branch of The Saddle Club. The girls had met her when they had visited their friend Kate Devine at her family's dude ranch, The Bar None, in Colorado. Christine lived near The Bar None.

"I bet she'd agree with me," Stevie said. "You know Christine. She's the type who would say that action speaks louder than plays."

"She'd probably hate all the corny Indian costumes, anyway," Lisa said thoughtfully. "You know how she feels about all that touristy stuff." When the girls had first met Christine, they had gotten off on the wrong foot with her by assuming that, because she was a Native American, she was always taking part in an ancient tribal ritual or something equally mysterious. Christine had soon set them straight on that point, but she still teased them about their misconceptions about Native Americans.

"Well, what kind of action did you have in mind, Stevie?" asked Carole. "I mean, our school is having a canned-food drive. . . ."

"Oh, come on," Stevie interrupted disdainfully. "You know what that means—all the kids will wait until the last minute, then go and grab all the cans out of the pantry that no one in their family wants to eat anyway. What's the good of foisting a bunch of cans of lima beans on some poor, unsuspecting person?"

Lisa and Carole exchanged another glance. They

11

could both tell that Stevie had something else in mind. When that was the case, it was practically impossible to guess just what that something was. The only thing to do was ask, so Lisa did. "What do you think we should do instead of lima beans and plays?"

"I'm glad you asked," Stevie said, rubbing her hands together eagerly. "I've been thinking about that, and I decided we should each try to do something that really reflects the meaning of Thanksgiving. Something generous and totally selfless."

"Like what?" Carole asked.

"Well, I'm not quite sure about that yet, but it has to be something that helps someone else without benefiting you at all," Stevie said. "You know how your parents always seem glad that the canned-food drive helps them clean out the pantry?" Lisa and Carole nodded. "Well, that's why it's no good," Stevie continued. "It's got to be something more selfless. Something that's maybe even a sacrifice on our part."

Carole shook her head. "I guess that's a good idea, but I still don't know exactly what I'm supposed to do."

"Me, neither," agreed Lisa.

"Well, I know I'm going to find something," Stevie said stubbornly. "And it's going to reflect the real meaning of Thanksgiving, like the kind and generous way the Native Americans acted when they helped the first Pilgrims stay alive. I don't know what it will be yet, but I'll figure something out before I leave for my relatives' house next week. You'll see." Like Carole and Lisa, Stevie and her three brothers had the following Thursday and Friday off from school for Thanksgiving, and their parents were taking them to visit Mrs. Lake's sister's family for the holiday.

"I'll try to find something to do, too," Lisa said. She didn't know what had brought about this philosophical streak in Stevie, but she had to admit that Stevie had a point when she said that people didn't do as much as they probably should to commemorate the first Thanksgiving.

"Me, too," Carole added. "It'll be a different kind of Saddle Club project."

Stevie's face lit up. "Great!" she exclaimed. "Even if everybody else thinks all they have to do to celebrate Thanksgiving is watch a play and eat some turkey, we'll show that that's not enough. We'll single-handedly—no, better make that triple-handedly—keep the meaning of Thanksgiving alive!"

"It's a deal," Carole said, and Lisa nodded. The Saddle Club clinked their mugs together and then settled back to finish their cocoa.

THE FOLLOWING MONDAY afternoon Carole hurried over to Pine Hollow right after school. The farrier was coming to put new shoes on some of the horses, including Starlight, and she didn't want to miss a thing.

Carole never passed up an opportunity to learn about anything having to do with horses. She already knew that she wanted to work with horses when she grew up, although she hadn't yet decided whether she would train them, own them, heal them, ride them, or all of the above.

In the meantime she wanted to learn everything she could about every aspect of horse care. It was easy for her to find a lot of opportunities to do so, mostly because there was a lot to learn. There were the everyday tasks that every rider at Pine Hollow was supposed to help out with, such as feeding and grooming and cleaning tack. There were the unexpected situations when a horse was injured or became sick. Carole had spent some time acting as an assistant to the local veterinarian, Judy Barker, and she had learned a lot that way about what a vet does. Finally, there were things like shoeing, which might seem a little boring to some people, but which Carole knew were important to keeping a horse healthy and happy. A horse's feet were more complicated than they looked, and it was vital to keep them in good shape.

Carole's thoughts on the subject were interrupted as she turned the corner into the stable entrance and almost ran into Veronica diAngelo.

"Oops! Sorry," Carole exclaimed. She had forgotten that Veronica's horse, Garnet, was also being shod that day. None of the other young riders from their class was at the stable, since it wasn't a regular lesson day. "I guess I wasn't watching where I was going."

Rather than the expected rude retort, Veronica merely nodded. "That's all right," she said.

Carole was surprised. Veronica was not known for her patience, and normally she didn't like it when anyone got in her way, literally or otherwise. "Are you here for Garnet's shoeing?" Carole asked. Now she remembered Lisa's saying that Max had insisted on Veronica's presence, but she was still a little surprised that Veronica had bothered to show up.

"Yes," Veronica replied. "Max is with the farrier now in Geronimo's stall. I think they're going to do Starlight next, then Garnet."

"Oh." Carole didn't quite know what to say to this new, polite Veronica. "Do you want to come and watch him do Starlight, then?"

The other girl shrugged. "Sure, why not."

The two of them walked off together in the direction of Starlight's stall. "Have you ever watched a horse being shod before?" Carole asked. Thinking about the reason they were both there almost made Carole forget that she was talking to Veronica. Her natural enthusiasm won out over her dislike of the snobbish girl.

Veronica shook her head. "I'm only here today because Max made me come," she said. But instead of sounding annoyed, her words came out as almost wistful.

Carole looked at her closely. "Are you all right?"

"Sure," Veronica said with another shrug. "Look, here we are."

Carole suspected that the other girl was trying to change the subject. She decided to let her, since they had reached Starlight's stall and Max was waiting for them there with the farrier.

"Hello, Carole, Veronica," Max greeted them. Carole thought she detected a quick look of surprise cross his face at seeing them together. But he recovered quickly and introduced Veronica to the farrier, a man named Alec McAllister. He had flaming red hair and a broad

16

smile. Carole had met him a few times before, since he came to give Starlight new shoes about once every four to six weeks, and Carole liked to be there to watch whenever she could.

"Good to meet you, Veronica. Howdy again, Carole," Alec said, briskly shaking first Veronica's hand, then Carole's. He looked over the stall door at Starlight, who was watching them all curiously. "And hello to you, too, Starlight. Remember me?"

"Of course he does," Carole told the farrier with a smile.

"All right, then, let's get to work," Alec exclaimed.

Carole brought Starlight out of his stall and cross-tied him in the wide passageway so that Alec would have plenty of room in which to work. When she had finished, Carole gave Starlight a pat on the neck and then stepped back so that Alec could get started.

As he worked, Alec chatted with Max about the other horses in the stable he would see that day. Since Alec was a traveling farrier who visited many stables and farms across a wide area, he could come to Pine Hollow only a couple of times per month. That meant he reshod some of Max's horses at each visit.

Carole noticed that Veronica was leaning back against the wall, arms crossed, looking a bit bored. She decided to explain some of what the farrier was doing, on the off chance that Veronica would be interested. "Watch this," Carole told her, nodding at Alec, who was bent over one of Starlight's front hooves. "See, he already removed Starlight's old shoes, and now he's checking his feet to make sure they're healthy."

Veronica shrugged noncommittally in response, and Carole took that as an invitation to keep talking.

"Okay, now he's going to trim off the dead material from the frogs of the feet," she said. "That's the rubbery part that juts into the back of the sole," she added. It was a fairly elementary anatomical term that Veronica certainly should know, but Carole knew that in Veronica's case it wasn't a good idea to take any knowledge for granted. Even though Veronica was a pretty good rider, she was just as lazy about things like learning horse anatomy as she was about mucking out Garnet's stall.

"I know what the frog is," Veronica replied a bit testily.

"Sorry," Carole said, trying not to smile. "Anyway, all he has to do is trim off the ragged edges around the frog to keep dirt from collecting there. But he has to be careful so he doesn't cut the healthy tissue underneath. Next he'll use a rasp to even out the edges of the hoof walls."

She paused for a moment to allow Alec's actions to catch up with her words. When he picked up the rasp, the farrier interrupted his conversation with Max about Topside's shoes and turned to Carole. "Carry on, instructor," he told her with a wink as Max grinned.

Carole blushed. The two men had been so involved in their conversation that she hadn't thought they'd even heard her. She was a little embarrassed that they had caught her lecturing Veronica on the shoeing process. But she also knew that she knew what she was talking about, so she continued.

"It's important that the force of the horse's weight and motion be distributed evenly on the foot," she explained as Alec started rasping. "After this, all that's left to do is attach the shoes, which have been specially fitted to Starlight's foot—"

"You mean horses have different-sized feet, just like people?" Veronica asked, showing the first glimmer of interest.

Carole wondered if that was because this was the first part of the process to which the fashion-conscious girl could really relate. She cast around for a way to explain that Veronica would understand. "Well, sure," she said. "It's like when you're at the mall trying on shoes, and they have all different sizes, you know?"

Veronica nodded eagerly. "I know," she said. "But it's so annoying when they don't have my size in the style I want. My mother says it happens so often because I have such small, delicate feet—"

"Uh-huh," Carole interrupted. She didn't want to get Veronica started on shopping—she was sure she could talk about that subject for just as long as Carole could talk about horses! "And the reason you want the shoes in your own size is because otherwise they'll be uncomfortable. They might give you blisters, make your feet really sore, and maybe even keep you from walking."

"I guess so," Veronica said dubiously. "But I usually just make someone drive me around to different stores until I find them in my size. Although once I wanted these great suede loafers, and no store in town had them in the right size, so Daddy had one of his friends mail them to me from New York." She smiled triumphantly at the memory.

Carole stifled a sigh. "Okay, but to get back to the subject at hand, it's even more important for a horse's shoe to fit properly than it is for yours. After all, a horse's shoe carries a lot more weight, and we all know how serious a leg injury can be." As soon as the last words left her mouth, Carole bit her lip, wishing she could take them back. Cobalt's death had been caused by a bad leg injury. Carole hoped Veronica didn't think she had been referring to that—even though Carole had to admit that it had been in the back of her mind.

Luckily, Veronica's mind seemed to be on something else entirely. "Right, right, so the shoe has to fit. I get it," she said impatiently.

"Well, then, to attach the shoe to the hoof, Alec will use nails and clips. The clips come already built into the shoes, and get hammered onto the walls of the foot. The nails go through the holes in the shoe into the horn." Just in time she stopped herself from explaining that the horn was the hard, insensitive outer part of the hoof.

"The horse can't feel it, any more than you feel it when you clip your fingernails. And that's it—the horse has new shoes."

"Hmmm," Veronica said. "I never realized how complicated the whole thing is."

Carole thought that there were probably a lot of complicated things Veronica didn't know about horse care—mostly because she never did any of them. But she knew that if she kept thinking about that, she'd just get angry and disgusted, and she didn't want that to happen now, when Veronica was being almost nice. So she decided to change the subject. "So, Veronica, what are you and your parents doing for Thanksgiving?" Carole asked.

Veronica frowned. "My parents are going to the Bahamas for the holiday weekend."

"Wow!" Carole said. Sometimes it was hard not to be impressed with Veronica's wealth. Carole's father made a comfortable enough living as a colonel in the Marine Corps, and he had recently taken her for a five-day vacation in Florida, but she couldn't imagine him ever whisking her off to the Bahamas for the weekend. "That's great. It's been so freezing lately; it's the perfect time to go. Have you ever been there before?"

"Yes, of course I have. But unfortunately I'm not going *this* time," Veronica said, sounding rather bitter. She gave Carole a sidelong glance. "I'm not invited."

"What?" Carole exclaimed. "But it's Thanksgiving!

How can your parents just take off and leave you behind?"

Carole realized almost immediately that it hadn't been the most tactful thing to say. She could tell by the look on Veronica's face that this was upsetting her more than her casual words let on. "You tell me," Veronica snapped.

"I'm sorry," Carole said quickly.

"That's all right," Veronica said. "It's not your fault that some stupid golfing trip is more important to my father than staying home for Thanksgiving."

"Why aren't they taking you with them?" Carole asked. "Then at least you'd be together for Thanksgiving." Carole knew that the diAngelos had more than enough money to be able to afford to bring Veronica with them. In fact, they had enough money to bring all of the riders at Pine Hollow with them to the Bahamas if they felt like it—and the horses, too!

"It's sort of a business trip," Veronica explained. "Some superimportant client of my father's has a vacation home down there, right next to some famous golf course. So he invited my father and his partner down. Their wives are invited, but not kids."

"That's terrible," Carole declared. "How could anyone separate families at this time of year?"

Veronica sighed. "Well, my father told me that this guy isn't American, he's British. So he probably didn't even realize when he planned this trip that it took place on Thanksgiving weekend."

"Oh, that explains it," Carole said, trying to make a joke. "He probably still carries a grudge about the Revolutionary War." She giggled at the thought that a modern Englishman would still be angry about America's victory over England more than two hundred years earlier.

But Veronica didn't even smile. Instead, she sighed again, more deeply this time. "Whatever the explanation, the result is that I get to spend Thanksgiving this year with the maid and the chauffeur."

Carole tried to look on the bright side of the situation. "I thought you liked them both a lot." Miles, the diAngelos' chauffeur, had picked Veronica up at Pine Hollow many times. He had always seemed very kind to Carole. After all, he was always nice to Veronica even when she was being impossibly difficult, which was most of the time.

"Oh, I do," Veronica said. "But they both have families, and I'm sure they'd much rather be with them for Thanksgiving than with me. They're only doing it because my father is paying them triple their ordinary salary for the weekend." She attempted a feeble smile. "It was an offer they couldn't refuse."

"Oh." Carole didn't know what to say next. She wished Lisa were there. She always seemed to know what to say to make people feel better. And Carole realized that she really did want to make Veronica feel better, despite all of The Saddle Club's efforts in the past to make her feel bad. Still, Carole remembered that every single one of those times there had been a reason for their scheming. Usually it was either because Veronica had been mistreating a horse, or because she'd been mistreating The Saddle Club.

This time was different. Carole had never before thought of Veronica diAngelo as vulnerable. After all, she seemed to have everything anyone could want, at least in terms of material things. She lived in a huge, elegant house, wore expensive designer riding clothes—including gorgeous leather boots that probably cost as much as Carole's entire wardrobe—and never had to worry about having enough spending money. Most important as far as Carole was concerned, she was the owner of Garnet, who in addition to being a beautiful, sweet-tempered horse, was also a purebred Arabian.

But the more Carole thought about it, the more she realized that she wouldn't want to trade places with Veronica for even one second. She had often noticed that the diAngelos seemed to try to solve every problem with money, even when it didn't really help at all. Whenever Veronica threw one of her frequent temper tantrums, her parents offered to buy her something to make her feel better. Carole suspected that this was because it was quicker than listening and trying to solve the real problem. She knew that Mr. diAngelo had an important job that took up a lot of his time.

Carole thought about her own father. Carole and her father had always been close, but since Mrs. Hanson's death a couple of years earlier, they had become closer than ever. Carole knew she could tell her father about anything that was bothering her, and that he would listen. In fact, her friends could count on Colonel Hanson to listen to their problems, too, and to help if he could.

That gave her an idea. If her father could help Stevie and Lisa with their problems, why not Veronica, too? And if Carole could get him to help Veronica to feel better, even though Carole didn't even *like* Veronica, it would be a true demonstration of selflessness—the perfect Thanksgiving project!

"Hey, Veronica," Carole blurted out, before she was really aware of what she was about to say. "Why don't you come spend the weekend with me and my father? I'm sure he wouldn't mind."

Veronica looked at her in surprise. For a second she looked suspicious, then thoughtful. She wrinkled her nose and opened her mouth as if to turn down the invitation, then stopped. Finally, she shrugged. "Well," she said, "I guess that might be better than nothing." She paused again. "In fact, it might even be fun or something." She smiled at Carole. "I'll call right now and ask my parents. I'm sure they'll say yes—I think they've been feeling guilty about the whole thing, anyway. Thanks a lot, Carole. I'm glad you asked."

"My pleasure. It'll be fun," Carole said weakly, wondering what she was letting herself in for. But there was no time to back out now.

"Max, can I use the phone in your office?" Veronica wheedled. "Pretty please?"

"Sure, go ahead," Max said. Normally, the phone in Max's office was reserved for emergencies. The riders were supposed to use the pay phone. But Carole suspected that Max was too surprised at hearing Veronica say "please" to insist on her following that rule. Either that, Carole thought ruefully, or he had overheard her own offer and was still in shock.

Carole bit her lip and tried to pay attention to what Alec was doing while she waited for Veronica to return. But her mind was racing, and for once she couldn't concentrate on the horse in front of her. She and her father had planned a quiet Thanksgiving dinner for just the two of them. After her mother's death Thanksgiving had become a quiet but very special time for Carole and her father. They used the day to remember her and be thankful for the time they'd had with her, and also to be thankful for having each other. This year they had been planning on spending the day cooking and eating together, then watching *Miracle on 34th Street* on television.

Even though Veronica was being much more human

today than usual, Carole had a difficult time imagining her fitting in with their modest plans. And what was more, she wasn't sure she *wanted* to imagine it.

Just then Veronica returned, breathless from running. "It's all set," she told Carole excitedly. "My parents said it's okay for me to stay with you. They'll drop me off here Wednesday on their way to the airport, and I can just go home with you when you come to take care of Starlight."

"Great," Carole said. "I can't wait." Suddenly she had another thought. What were Stevie and Lisa going to say? Carole almost groaned out loud. She had a feeling she was in for a whole lot of teasing from her friends. Still, she reminded herself, she was supposed to find something generous and selfless to do to celebrate Thanksgiving. And watching Veronica's happy expression, Carole knew that her invitation had made the other girl feel much better.

And that's what the spirit of Thanksgiving is all about, Carole thought. Isn't it?

THE NEXT DAY, Tuesday, Carole arrived at Pine Hollow about forty minutes before class. She hadn't told either Stevie or Lisa yet about her new Thanksgiving project. She was wishing by this point that she could somehow go back in time and take back her offer to Veronica. But there was no way she could back out of it now—especially when she remembered the grateful look on the other girl's face when she'd accepted.

When Carole had told her father about her invitation to Veronica, he had immediately okayed the idea. In fact, he had seemed excited about it. That's only because he doesn't know Veronica very well, Carole thought wryly. Colonel Hanson was a parent sponsor of Pine Hollow's Pony Club, Horse Wise, so he had met Veronica plenty of times. But he didn't know her well enough to know how rotten she could be when things didn't go her way.

Carole hadn't called Stevie or Lisa the night before to tell them her news. And even though Carole and Lisa went to the same school, they were in different grades and hadn't seen each other all day.

Usually when Carole had a problem, she told her friends about it right away. They all took very seriously the Saddle Club rule about helping each other, and Carole knew she could count on Stevie and Lisa for anything, large or small. But Carole really didn't think there was much either she or her friends could do about this particular problem. Unless she—or Veronica—came down with a major disease in the next few days, they would be spending Thanksgiving weekend together, for better or for worse. Besides, Carole couldn't help thinking that Stevie was at least a little bit to blame for the whole situation. After all, if it wasn't for Stevie's Thanksgiving-project idea, Carole probably wouldn't even have considered trying to help Veronica.

Carole grinned for a second, wondering if she could make Stevie feel guilty enough to offer to take Veronica along on the Lakes' vacation. Then she sighed. Stevie and Lisa would be arriving at the stable soon, and she was just going to have to bite the bullet and tell them what she'd done, even though she knew she was going to get some teasing. No, make that a *lot* of teasing.

But first, she had a good excuse to put it off a little bit

longer. The last time she'd untacked Starlight, she had noticed that one of the stirrup leathers on his saddle was starting to look worn. She had made sure to arrive a little early today so she'd have time to replace it, and the other one as well. If one leather was wearing out, she knew it wouldn't be long before the other one would, too. The leather holding the left-hand stirrup always got more wear and tended to stretch out more since riders always mounted and dismounted from the left side, but Carole, like most conscientious riders, made sure to switch the leathers from side to side so they would get the same amount of wear—and remain the same length. But now it was time to change them both, and Carole didn't want to put it off. Having a stirrup leather break while in the saddle was always a nuisance, and sometimes a danger.

She headed toward the tack room. When she arrived, she was so intent on her task that she almost didn't notice that the door to Mrs. Reg's office, which adjoined the tack room on one side, was slightly ajar. Even if she had noticed, she wouldn't have thought anything of it. But as Carole was digging around in the trunk full of extra stirrup leathers, she heard a male voice coming from behind the door. She paused and listened long enough to determine that the voice belonged to Max, who seemed to be talking animatedly to someone on the phone. Then she turned her attention back to the leathers. It was a little unusual for Max to use the phone in his mother's office rather than his own, but it was certainly nothing to worry about.

Then Carole heard something that made her forget all about stirrup leathers. Was she going crazy, or had Max just said something about a "lovely lady"—and then *giggled*?

Max was a good friend to the riders he taught, including The Saddle Club. But Carole had to admit that they didn't know much about his personal life. In fact, now that she stopped to think about it, she had always sort of assumed that he didn't really have one outside Pine Hollow. Now she realized that that might not be a fair assumption. After all, at the moment it sounded as though Max was talking to someone about a woman!

Carole dropped the handful of leathers she was holding and scooted as close to the office door as she dared. For a moment she felt guilty about eavesdropping, but Max's next words made her forget those feelings entirely.

"Great, then everything's settled," Max was saying. "Provided I can get someone to take care of things here for a few days, tell Lillian I hope I'll be seeing her soon." He chuckled. "And tell that special lady that I really hope she'll be coming home with me after the visit!"

Carole gasped, then belatedly clapped her hand over her mouth, hoping Max hadn't heard her. A special lady, whom Max wanted to bring home with him? It could mean only one thing—Max was in love! She couldn't believe he hadn't let on a thing about it before this. It was so romantic!

But she didn't have much of a chance to think about it. She could hear Max saying good-bye and hanging up the phone. The legs of Mrs. Reg's old wooden chair were scraping against the floor. In a second Carole knew that Max would come out and see her there, and he would surely realize that she must have heard his conversation. If he had just been discussing grain prices or something, it wouldn't have mattered, but Carole was afraid he'd be embarrassed, or even angry, if he knew she'd overheard him making plans to see his girlfriend. And if he was planning to bring this woman back to Pine Hollow with him and nobody had heard about it, he must have wanted to keep it a secret. Maybe Mrs. Reg didn't even know about it! Maybe Max and his special lady were planning to elope! Maybe—

But Carole didn't have time for any more *maybe*'s just then. She glanced frantically at the tack-room door, wondering if she should make a run for it. The trouble was, if she shut the heavy, squeaky lid of the old metal trunk containing the stirrup leathers, Max would hear it and know she'd been there. And if she left it open, she was certain he'd be so annoyed at this bit of carelessness that he'd be sure to track down who had done it. She was trapped!

Just then her gaze fell on something lying on a low shelf near the door. It was Red's portable radio and headphones. Carole knew that the stable hand sometimes liked to listen to music while he cleaned tack to make the tedious job go faster. Luckily, he must have forgotten and left it behind after his last cleaning session. Moving quickly, Carole tiptoed across the floor, grabbed the tiny radio, and jammed the headphones on her ears. She just had time to turn it on, twist the volume knob to "loud," and sit down again in front of the trunk full of stirrup leathers before Max stepped out of Mrs. Reg's office with a big smile on his face.

He seemed startled to see her there. "Oh—hello, Carole," he said pleasantly. He didn't seem too concerned that she might have overheard him, and Carole silently congratulated herself for the radio idea.

She pretended to be surprised to see him, too. "Oh, hi, Max. I didn't know you were in there." She gave a little wave and then continued to sort through the leathers, swaying and nodding her head in time to the music.

"Uh, yes, I was just making a phone call," Max replied. He looked a little puzzled as he stared at the headphones. "Is that Red's radio?"

"What did you say? I can't hear you with these headphones on," Carole said loudly. Actually she could hear him perfectly well, even over the loud country-and-western music that was blaring out of the headphones. She figured it was better to be on the safe side, though, and make him think she couldn't hear a thing. She was sure that Stevie, who was famous for her schemes, would be proud of her for adding this extra detail.

Max stepped over to her and lifted the headphones off her head. The sound of a woman with a strong southern accent crooning something about standing by her man came out of them, sounding a bit tinny because of the small size of the headphones. Max was starting to look a bit suspicious. "Since when are you a fan of country music, Carole?" he asked, switching the radio off.

She shrugged. "Oh, I don't know," she said nervously. "I guess I just have varied tastes."

Max said something that sounded like "hmmph," but he seemed satisfied with her answer. "Well, don't get so caught up in your tunes that you're late for class." With that he left the room, and Carole breathed a sigh of relief.

Then she grinned. She couldn't wait to tell Stevie and Lisa what she'd heard. Max had a girlfriend! This was really big news.

Suddenly she remembered that she still had one other piece of news to tell them about: Project Veronica. Carole groaned. Teasing or no teasing, there was no point in keeping it from them any longer. Trying to be optimistic, she thought that Stevie might even be proud of her for taking on such a task.

As if reading her thoughts, Stevie's first words when she saw Carole were, "Hi, Carole. Have you come up with a Thanksgiving project yet?"

Carole gulped. She'd planned on easing her friends into the news slowly. "Um, as a matter of fact, I have," she said.

"Really?" Stevie looked excited. "Lisa and I were just talking about ideas, but we haven't come up with anything good. So what's yours?"

Carole decided that the best thing to do was just to blurt it out. So she did. "I invited Veronica to spend Thanksgiving weekend at my house," she said all in one breath.

Stevie and Lisa stared at her for a moment as if she'd lost her mind. Then they both started laughing. "Good one, Carole," Stevie chortled. "I almost believed you for a minute!"

It took some doing, but Carole finally convinced them that she was serious. She explained the situation with Veronica's parents. "I just felt sorry for her, having to spend the holiday practically alone," she said.

"Well, you're the one I feel sorry for," Stevie declared.

"Stevie's right," Lisa agreed. "I think you may be taking this selflessness thing too far. Spending that much time with Veronica has got to be the ultimate sacrifice!"

"Yeah, the meaning of Thanksgiving is one thing. This could get you qualified for sainthood or something," Stevie added, only half joking.

Carole sighed. "I know, I know. But you should have seen Veronica yesterday. She was actually being—well—*nice*."

"I don't believe it," Stevie said flatly. "All I can say is, I'm glad it's not me who has to deal with her. In fact, I'm glad I'll be far away at my relatives' house during the whole thing. I don't even want to have to watch *you* deal with her."

Carole decided it was time to distract her friends from the subject of Veronica. Luckily, she had the perfect way to do it. "Never mind Veronica," she said. "I'll put up with her somehow. But have I got news for you!" Quickly, she filled them in on what she'd overheard.

"I can't believe it!" Lisa exclaimed when Carole had finished. "Our Max has a girlfriend?"

Stevie thought Lisa sounded a little like a proud parent, and she told her so. "Not that I blame you," she added. "It *is* pretty exciting to think of Max being in love—maybe even getting married! From what you heard, Carole, it sounds like he wants to bring this Lillian woman back here with him, maybe permanently. Just think, we could be having another wedding at Pine Hollow before too long!" The past April Fool's Day, Stevie had planned a mock wedding between two of the horses at Pine Hollow, a stallion named Geronimo and a mare named Delilah. At the last minute the fake wedding had been turned into a real wedding to save the day for a human couple.

"Or eloping," Carole said. "That's my guess. I bet Mrs. Reg doesn't even know." She sighed wistfully. "Lillian is such a pretty name."

Lisa, always the practical one of the group, brought them back down to earth. "We shouldn't blow this out of proportion," she cautioned them. "After all, from what you heard, we don't know how serious things are. This could even be Max's first date with this woman."

"Well, maybe," Carole said doubtfully. "But Max sounded pretty serious about her on the phone. I mean, he said he wanted to bring her back here with him. I wonder exactly when he's going to visit her. . . . He didn't really say; he just said he'd see her soon."

"It was smart of you not to let on that you'd heard," Stevie told Carole. "If he knew we knew about it, we'd never be able to find out anything from him. This way he won't be suspicious, so if we ask him the right questions, maybe . . ." She let her voice trail off mysteriously, but her friends knew what she meant. Maybe they could find out more about Max's mystery woman, Lillian.

"I think finding out all we can about Max's new romance should be our next Saddle Club project," Carole declared.

"I definitely agree," Stevie said. "I just wish I had an idea of what to do for my part of our other project. I'm leaving for my aunt's house tomorrow, and I still haven't come up with anything good at all. I just can't think of anything to do."

"Me, neither," Lisa said. "But I do have a pretty good idea of what we should be doing right now, and that's tacking up our horses. We only have fifteen minutes until class starts."

Carole glanced at her watch. "Uh-oh, you're right. Let's go!" The girls hurried off in separate directions to get their horses ready for riding class. Fifteen minutes was plenty of time to tack up a horse, but they didn't want to take a chance of being late. They all knew how annoyed Max got when someone was late for class, and they also knew that they liked him a lot better when he *wasn't* annoyed.

AT THE END of class that day, Max announced that he had a favor to ask. "As you all know," he began, "Thanksgiving is this week. I know most of you have some time off from school, and a lot of you probably have special plans with your families. I was hoping to make a pretty special trip myself to visit a good friend, but I'm having some problems arranging it."

Stevie glanced furtively at Lisa and Carole. They both knew what she was thinking, because they were both thinking the same thing: This must be the special trip to visit Lillian that Carole had just overheard Max planning on the phone!

"In any case," Max was saying, "Red won't be able to do all the work himself, and I'm having trouble finding anyone who wants to work. I know it's short notice, but if any of you knows anyone with stable experience who would be willing to work then, please let me know as soon as possible. Thanks, and that's all for today. Class dismissed."

Stevie untacked and groomed her horse, Topside, as quickly as possible. She checked to make sure his stall was clean and everything was in order. No matter how rushed Stevie might be, or how careless she was about some things, she knew how important it was to make sure her horse was properly taken care of. But that didn't necessarily mean that she always had to spend a *lot* of time on it—especially when she had such important things to discuss with her friends!

Finally, she finished and hurried to Starlight's stall. Lisa had already joined Carole there. "Did you guys hear that?" Stevie asked breathlessly. She joined Lisa in leaning over the bottom half of Starlight's stall door so she could talk to Carole, who was inside grooming him.

Lisa nodded. "He had to be talking about his visit to Lillian. Isn't it romantic?"

"Totally," Carole agreed. "The problem is, it doesn't sound as if Max is going to be able to visit her after all. It'll be practically impossible for him to find someone to help out on such short notice, especially over a holiday weekend."

"You're right," Stevie said, her eyes sparkling. "That's why Max is so lucky he has us to help him!"

Carole shrugged as she ran a soft brush down Starlight's neck. "You know we'll do whatever we can to help him, but I can't think of a single person to ask."

"Well, I can't either, not right now," Stevie admitted. "But we have to think of someone. We just have to." She bit her lip anxiously, hoping she'd be able to come up with a solution to Max's problem before she left for her aunt's house the following afternoon.

"You know, I never thought much about it before, but Max really has a twenty-four-hours-per-day, seven-days-a-week job, doesn't he?" Lisa mused.

"He really does," Carole agreed. "Owning a stable is a big responsibility. All the horses here depend on him. I guess it's pretty hard to get time off."

"And all Max wants is a few days off to go visit his beloved girlfriend," Stevie said with a sigh. "It doesn't seem like much to ask." She thought about what it would be like if she didn't ever have time to see her own boyfriend, Phil Marsten, and decided she definitely wouldn't like it. Stevie and Phil had met at riding camp, and even though he lived in a town about twenty minutes' drive from Willow Creek, they managed to see each other at least once or twice a month.

"Well, even if we don't have any ideas right now, I think we should try to help Max somehow," Lisa said.

The others nodded in agreement.

Before they left the stable, Lisa told her friends that she wanted to go check on Pepper. She was still worried about his strange behavior the other day, and she wanted to see if staying inside had helped him return to normal.

"I'll meet you out front in a few minutes," Stevie said. "I'm going to talk to some of the others from class about Max's problem. Maybe someone has more of an idea than we do."

"I'll come with you," Carole offered. She and Stevie headed for the locker area of the stable, where the riders stowed their belongings.

Lisa walked off toward Pepper's stall. Even before she arrived, she knew something was amiss. Usually, as soon as anyone turned into the long passageway that formed one side of the U-shaped row of stalls, the old horse was at the front of his stall, looking for attention. But now, even though Barq and Garnet and several other horses were watching Lisa's approach, Pepper's gentle gray face was nowhere to be seen. When Lisa reached his stall, she could see why. Pepper was standing with his head hanging low, facing the back corner of the stall. He barely seemed to know that Lisa was there. The only sign that he noticed her at all was that one ear flicked slowly back as she approached.

"How does he look?"

Lisa was concentrating so hard on Pepper that she didn't notice that Max was behind her until he spoke.

She turned around. "Not so good," she said worriedly. "Last week I thought it was just the cold weather that was making him so listless. But he doesn't seem much better now that he's inside. Do you think he's sick?"

"I've been worried about Pepper, too. That's why I

41

asked Judy Barker to look at him the last time she was here."

"What did she say?" Lisa asked. Carole had told her friends lots of stories about the vet's work, and the way she had healed horses with all kinds of seemingly mysterious ailments. Lisa hoped Judy could do the same for Pepper.

But Max was shaking his head. "She didn't feel there was much to be done. Pepper is old. Very old. He's just getting tired out."

Lisa knew that since his retirement, Pepper hadn't had as much energy as he used to. She figured that she'd just have to get used to this calmer personality of his. Besides, Pepper had been staying inside for only a few days, and he had spent one night out in freezing temperatures. It would probably take him a while to recover from that, especially at his age. She just wished that she had thought to ask Max to bring Pepper inside earlier, as soon as it had started getting chilly at night.

Still, she thought that Judy should be doing something for Pepper other than calling him old. "Did she give you any medicine for him or anything?" she asked.

Max put one hand on Lisa's shoulder. "The only medicine Pepper needs right now is to know that he still has friends like you who care about him."

"Oh, I do," Lisa replied fervently. "I'll make sure he knows it." As Max headed back to his office, Lisa picked up a body brush and let herself into Pepper's stall. Talking gently to the old horse, she started to groom his already spotless coat. She knew that most horses, including Pepper, enjoyed being groomed whether they needed it or not. They just liked the attention and the feel of the brushes. Lisa had often thought of it as being a lot like a massage. Now she made sure she took special care to hit all of the spots Pepper most liked scratched.

By the time she left Pepper's stall, Lisa was sure that the old horse looked happier than he had when she'd arrived. He even moved to the front of the stall and watched as she walked away. She knew that, because she turned around at the end of the hallway to blow him a kiss. He gave a little nicker, as if he understood what she was doing.

Lisa smiled as she headed outside to meet her friends. Max was right. All Pepper needed was more attention. He had probably been bored out there in the pasture by himself all the time. She vowed to spend some time with him whenever she came to Pine Hollow.

THAT NIGHT AT the dinner table at Stevie's house, the talk was all about Thanksgiving and the Lakes' upcoming trip to visit Mrs. Lake's sister and her family in Darlington, Maryland. They were leaving the next afternoon right after school. Stevie had been so busy at Pine Hollow lately that she hadn't started packing yet, but she figured she'd do it right after dinner. Stevie never wasted much time on boring things like packing.

Stevie always looked forward to this yearly trip, despite the fact that her aunt's Thanksgiving dinner had to be among the worst in the country. Aside from the turkey and stuffing, the whole dinner always consisted entirely of root vegetables—turnips, parsnips, rutabagas, and the like. Over the years, Stevie and her brothers had

44

devised plenty of ingenious ways of slipping the worst of these vegetables to the family dogs.

Even though Thanksgiving dinner didn't rank high on Stevie's list of fun things in life, seeing her cousins definitely did. There were three of them, and they were all girls, which meant that for once Stevie's brothers were outnumbered.

Stevie's other favorite thing about the trip was going to the Darlington Fall Festival, a small country fair that was held every year on the Saturday and Sunday after Thanksgiving. The Festival had plenty of game booths and raffles and contests, and even a few carnival rides. The local residents set up tables to sell handcrafted items and homemade baked goods and preserves. There was a farm show, with prizes for the largest produce and the healthiest animals. On Saturday night there was a big dance called the Festival Frolic.

In Stevie's opinion the best part of the fair was the amateur horse show that was held on Sunday afternoon. Actually, it was part horse show, part rodeo, part free-for-all—and all fun. The entrants ranged from five-year-olds on Shetland ponies to experienced riders on Thoroughbreds to little old ladies riding sidesaddle on giant farm horses.

The most popular event in the show was undoubtedly the costume parade. The audience had to guess what each horse and rider was supposed to be, and then vote on the best costumes. The previous year the blue ribbon had gone to a girl a little younger than Stevie. She had ridden out into the ring dressed all in red, with fronds of greenery sprouting from her hard hat. Stevie had been the first to figure out that the girl was supposed to be a radish—and that because she was on horseback, naturally that made her a horseradish! Stevie was pretty sure that her aunt had appreciated the girl's costume, too. After all, radishes were one of her favorite vegetables.

All in all, Stevie thought that there were only a couple of bad things about the costume parade and the other equestrian events. One was that she couldn't participate in them herself, since her relatives didn't own any horses. The other was that Carole and Lisa couldn't be there to enjoy it with her. Still, the Festival was one of the things that made Thanksgiving special to Stevie.

"I wish I could be in the costume contest," Stevie remarked wistfully. "I'd win first prize for sure. I have a million great ideas."

Her twin brother, Alex, snorted. "You and your one-track mind. There's more to the Festival than the horse show, you know. For instance, you can watch me win all the prizes at the dart-balloon booth." He pretended to wind up and throw a dart, aiming at Stevie's head.

"In your dreams," Stevie shot back. "You know I beat you at that booth every time we played last year." It was true. Stevie had ended up with a giant stuffed bear, while Alex had only been able to win some plastic cars and a key chain.

"I like the duck game the best," announced Michael, Stevie's youngest brother. "It's easy to win."

"Right," Stevie said. "All you have to do to win a prize is pick up a plastic duck. Maybe Alex should try it. Even he couldn't lose."

"Funny," Alex said. Checking to make sure Mr. and Mrs. Lake weren't looking, he opened his mouth as wide as he could, displaying the partially chewed contents to Stevie. Michael and Chad, Stevie's oldest brother, laughed.

She ignored them. "Mom, what's your favorite part of the Festival?" she asked, putting some more salad onto her plate.

"Well, I do like the dance," she said. "But the best part of the weekend for me isn't the Festival, it's seeing your aunt. Considering that we don't live very far apart, it seems as though I hardly ever get to spend time with her."

"Who says we don't live far apart?" Alex protested. "All I know is it takes practically forever to get to their house."

"It certainly seems to take forever when I have to spend the whole trip trapped in the car with them," Stevie said, gesturing at her brothers.

"I don't even care if I have to sit by Stevie the whole way. The trip is going to be a blast this year. I can't wait to get there," said Chad dreamily. Chad was two years older than Stevie, and the year before, he had met a girl named Ellen, who was a friend of their cousin Mia's. Chad and Ellen had really hit it off, and they had been exchanging letters and phone calls for the past year. Chad always insisted that she wasn't really his girlfriend, but it was obvious that he liked her a lot.

Stevie and Alex exchanged a look, then started chanting in unison, "Chad and Ellen, sitting in a tree, K-I-S-S-I—"

"That's enough, you two," Mr. Lake interrupted. Stevie would have sworn her father was trying to hold back a smile. "Stop teasing your brother."

"Stevie," Mrs. Lake said, obviously trying to change the subject, "I'm sure you're looking forward to the Festival this year."

"Sure, Mom," Stevie said distractedly. Thinking about Chad and Ellen had reminded her of another romantic couple—namely, Max and his mystery woman, Lillian. And that reminded her that unless The Saddle Club could come up with a solution to Max's personnel problem, it was likely that Max wouldn't be able to see his girlfriend that weekend at all.

Suddenly the perfect solution popped into Stevie's mind. She was so excited that she almost choked on the mouthful of peas she was eating. After gulping down some water, she was able to speak. "Mom, Dad? I have an idea," she said, trying to sound as mature as possible. She didn't have time to think of the best way to approach them with the idea. She'd just have to tell them her plan and hope for the best.

Her parents looked at her, surprised by the serious tone of her voice. "Yes, Stevie? What is it?" her mother asked.

"Well, you see, Max has this problem. He has a very special friend he wants to visit this weekend, but he can't go unless he can find someone to help Red at the stable."

"And?" Mr. Lake said expectantly. Although Stevie's parents claimed to disapprove of most of Stevie's schemes, she suspected that they often rather enjoyed hearing them. However, she also knew that just because they listened to them didn't guarantee that they would be willing to go along with them.

She took a deep breath. "I was thinking, Max hardly ever gets time off, and he deserves a vacation for a change. And Carole and Lisa and I were just talking about the meaning of Thanksgiving the other day—"

She was interrupted by a snort from Chad. "I bet you were. The meaning of Thanksgiving according to you guys must have something to do with horses. Let me guess, you decided that the real reason the Pilgrims came to America was because we have better riding trails."

"Chad," Mr. Lake said warningly.

Normally Stevie would have come back with an insult of her own, but right now she didn't want anything to distract her. So she just gave her brother a withering look, then turned back to her parents.

"Anyway, we decided that the best way to celebrate Thanksgiving was by doing something to help someone else, you know, without thinking of yourself at all," she said earnestly. "Something generous and totally selfless."

Mr. and Mrs. Lake looked at each other in surprise. "What a lovely thought, Stevie," Mrs. Lake said. "But what exactly did you have in mind?"

"I want to stay here this weekend and help out so Max can go on his trip," Stevie said. "After all, practically no one knows the stable and the horses better than I do. And I'm pretty sure I can stay at Lisa's house while you guys are gone. They're just having Thanksgiving dinner at home this year." No matter how selfless she was being, Stevie didn't consider staying with Carole for a single moment. There was no way she was staying in the same house as Veronica!

Mr. Lake looked thoughtful. "But what about the Fall Festival? I thought you loved that."

"Oh, I do," Stevie said. "But that's what Thanksgiving is about, isn't it? Helping other people, even if you have to give up some things to do it."

"Well, Stevie, I'm proud of you," Mrs. Lake said.

"For wanting to help Max, you mean?" Stevie said.

Mrs. Lake chuckled. "Well, that too. But mostly I'm proud of you for just coming out and asking us about this, instead of concocting some sort of devious plan to trick us into agreeing to it."

Stevie didn't know quite how to answer that, so she just smiled. She also crossed her fingers under the table. Her parents hadn't actually said yes yet, and now that she'd come up with this idea, Stevie knew it was an absolutely perfect Thanksgiving project.

"Well, I think she's crazy to want to pass up this trip," Alex announced.

"Me, too," Michael piped up.

Chad didn't say anything. Stevie glanced at him and saw that he was gazing down into his mashed potatoes with a goofy smile on his face. He was slowly stirring the potatoes and humming softly. Stevie was sure he was thinking about Ellen, but she resisted the strong urge to tease him and looked back at her parents. They were both still looking thoughtful.

"Please, Mom and Dad," Stevie said. "This means a lot to me."

Her parents exchanged another glance. "We'll think about it, Stevie," Mr. Lake said. "And we will take your sincerity into account."

"Thanks," Stevie said, with what she hoped was an encouraging smile. This was the first time she could remember trying the straightforward approach with anything this important. She couldn't believe it, but it seemed to be working.

*　*　*

AFTER DINNER STEVIE called Lisa and told her about her plan. Lisa checked with her parents, who said they'd be happy to have Stevie stay there. Lisa also promised to help pitch in at the stable herself.

Stevie found her parents relaxing in the den and told them what the Atwoods had said. "So what do you say?" she asked, holding her breath while she waited for their answer.

Mr. Atwood set down the magazine he was reading. "Well, Stevie, we've discussed it. We know that you must really want to help Max if you're willing to give up the trip to Maryland for him."

"That's right," Stevie agreed eagerly. "Max does so much for me all year long, I just thought he needed his trip more than I need mine."

"All right, Stevie," Mrs. Atwood said. "If it means that much to you, you have our permission."

"Oh, great!" Stevie exclaimed, giving both her parents giant bear hugs. "Thanks a million! I've got to go call Max and tell him the good news right away."

She rushed into the kitchen to call Max and volunteer her services as an assistant stable hand. At first she had a hard time convincing him that, first of all, she was serious about it, and second of all, she had already cleared it with her parents. But after she put Mrs. Lake on the phone to confirm it, Max was full of gratitude.

"I really appreciate this, Stevie," he said. "This trip is very important to me, and for a while there it was looking as though my mother and I weren't going to be able to go."

Stevie was surprised to hear that Mrs. Reg was going along with Max on his romantic visit. That seemed to disprove Carole's theory about an elopement. Maybe Lisa was right and this was a first date, and maybe Mrs. Reg had arranged it. Stevie decided that this was just one more mysterious detail they would have to investigate.

"It's all set," Stevie told her parents after she finished talking to Max and hung up the phone. "Max leaves tomorrow morning."

"I hope you realize, Stevie, you've taken on a big responsibility," Mr. Lake said. "Max is really counting on you."

"I know," Stevie said. "It'll be even more work than that time Carole and Lisa and I took over for Mrs. Reg when she had to go see her sick friend." She smiled at the memory. That time The Saddle Club had misinterpreted some of Mrs. Reg's instructions and had ended up doing more work than they really had to because of it. But everything had turned out all right in the end, and Stevie was sure she'd learned a lot from the experience. That knowledge would come in handy now, especially with both Max *and* Mrs. Reg away. "But it'll be fun. I can't wait."

"Well, we'll miss you," Mrs. Lake said. She paused. "Most of us, anyway."

Stevie rolled her eyes. "If you're referring to my dear brothers, let me assure you I won't miss them either."

"That's not who I meant," Mrs. Lake said with a mischievous smile. "I was just thinking that your aunt Louise will probably be relieved not to have a replay of last year's parsnip incident."

"Oh, that," Stevie said, giggling. It had been one of her finest moments. At Thanksgiving dinner the year before, Stevie had put a parsnip on her linen napkin and jerked the napkin tight to make the parsnip jump up. It had jumped a little higher than she had been expecting and had ended up mashed on the ceiling. It had remained there, much to her aunt's dismay, until dessert, when it had dislodged itself and plopped back down—right into Chad's pumpkin pie.

RIGHT AFTER SCHOOL the next day, Stevie's parents dropped her off at Lisa's house on their way out of town. Stevie took her suitcase up to Lisa's room, then the two girls set off for Pine Hollow. Stevie couldn't wait to get started in her role of assistant stable hand. For her part, Lisa was glad she'd be able to help Stevie with her Thanksgiving project, although she hadn't had any luck so far figuring out what to do for her own. She was beginning to worry that she'd never find a project in time, since Thanksgiving was the next day.

When they arrived at the stable, one of the first things they noticed was how quiet it was. There were no other people around, as there usually were at almost any time of the day, any day of the week. Everyone seemed to have deserted Pine Hollow for the holiday. But Stevie and Lisa knew that there had to be at least one other person there: Carole. They knew their friend well enough to know that she would be there, taking care of Starlight as usual, holiday or no holiday.

And they were right. They found Carole in Starlight's stall, hoof pick in hand, cleaning out his feet.

"Hi, you two. Are you ready for your new jobs?" Carole asked. Stevie had called her the night before to tell her about her plan.

"You bet," Stevie said, sliding open the door to Starlight's stall and stepping inside. Lisa was right behind her. One of the things that made taking care of horses so much fun was that there was so much of them to take care of. That meant that all three girls could groom Starlight at once—and talk while they were doing it, of course. They had held plenty of impromptu Saddle Club meetings this way in the past, and today's grooming seemed to be turning into another one.

Stevie picked up a wide-toothed comb and set to work on the gelding's dark, silky mane, carefully loosening tangles and picking out pieces of hay. "I'm really looking forward to it," she said in response to Carole's question.

"We'll probably learn a lot," Lisa agreed, grabbing a body brush.

Stevie grinned. "Right. But the best part is, we'll know we're doing it all for Max and his love life."

"You know I'll pitch in as much as I can," Carole said, setting aside the hoof pick and picking up a rub rag. "But

I don't know how easy it will be to convince Veronica to help." Since Veronica was so famous for getting out of doing her own chores, Carole certainly couldn't imagine her volunteering to take on anybody else's.

"Oh, yeah," Stevie said, wrinkling her nose in distaste. "Well, I still think you've taken on the toughest job of all by volunteering to baby-sit Veronica for the whole weekend. I bet she'll be more work than this whole stable full of horses. I mean, she'll probably expect you and your father to bring her breakfast in bed every day, polish her boots for her, that kind of thing."

"Shh," Carole whispered, glancing out at the corridor. "She's here someplace. She came to take care of Garnet."

"You mean she's actually doing some work?" Stevie said in disbelief.

Lisa smiled. "I guess Carole's being a good influence already. Maybe there's hope for Veronica yet."

"I think there might be," Carole said. "I've never seen her be as pleasant as she's been for the past few days." She gave Starlight's coat a last once-over with the cloth in her hand. She double-checked his food and water and then gave him a pat before leaving the stall. Her friends followed. "I guess I'll find out soon enough," Carole added quietly as she spotted Veronica heading toward them from the other end of the corridor. "My father is picking us up in a few minutes."

"Lucky you," Stevie muttered. She gave Veronica

what she hoped was a sincere-looking smile as the girl approached. Stevie noticed that Veronica had a small but expensive-looking leather suitcase slung casually over her shoulder by a long strap. In one hand she was carrying a matching square case that Stevie would have been willing to bet contained her makeup. In the other hand she was holding a suspiciously pie-shaped object wrapped in aluminum foil. "Hi, Veronica."

"Hi, Stevie. Hi, Lisa," Veronica responded. Stevie could tell that she, too, was doing her best to be pleasant and not show that she didn't like Stevie any more than Stevie liked her. "Ready to go, Carole?" she asked sweetly.

"Sure," Carole replied. "My dad should be here by now. Let's go out and check."

"Okay," Veronica said agreeably. "I hope you and your dad like pumpkin pie," she added, holding up the foil-wrapped package. "Our cook baked this especially for you."

"That was awfully nice of you, Veronica," Carole said sincerely. She giggled. "My dad is a great cook, but he's not much of a baker. You've probably just saved us all from a repeat of the great Apple Pie Horror from last year."

Stevie and Lisa watched in silence as Carole and Veronica walked off together, chatting easily. When they were out of sight, Stevie let out a long sigh that ended in a whistle. "I hope Carole survives this holiday," she commented.

"I'm sure she'll be fine," Lisa replied with a smile. She didn't like Veronica much better than Stevie did, but she had to admit that Veronica seemed to be trying to be nice. And she admired Carole for giving her the benefit of the doubt.

Just then Red came hurrying up to them. "Oh, Stevie, there you are. I have a job for you."

Stevie snapped to attention and gave a mock salute. "Aye, aye, Captain. At your service. What do you need me to do?"

Red gazed at her in amusement. "It's a pretty exciting job, First Mate Lake," he said.

"Great, what is it?" Stevie asked. "Exercising one of the horses? Straightening out the tack room? Hosing down the floors?"

"Mucking out the stalls," Red replied drily.

"Oh." Stevie tried not to groan. She reminded herself that this wasn't really supposed to be fun. In fact, it was supposed to be a sacrifice. That made her feel a little better. It almost, but not quite, made mucking out stalls seem exotic. "Lead on, Captain," she said, sounding almost as enthusiastic as before.

Lisa smiled and shook her head. Stevie could make almost anything seem like fun, even something like mucking out stalls. "Do you need me to help?" she asked.

"No, I don't think so," Red said. "We actually don't have many to do right now. But I may take you up on the offer later."

"Good," Lisa said. "Then in the meantime I'm going to check on Pepper. Have fun, Stevie!" Lisa was determined to stick to her vow to buck up the old horse's spirits by keeping him company. She was sure Max had been right when he'd said it would make Pepper feel better.

When Lisa arrived at the stall, Pepper once again failed to greet her at the door. She slipped into the stall, talking to him quietly so that he wouldn't be startled by her approach.

"Hi, boy," she said gently. "Are you feeling better today?" Almost immediately, Lisa could tell that the answer to her question was a negative one. Pepper's head was hanging lower than ever, and he seemed to be having difficulty breathing. But he still seemed happy to see her, and Lisa was glad that she'd taken the time to visit with him.

Pepper turned his head to nuzzle Lisa's pants pocket. She laughed. "Now I know there can't be anything that bad wrong with you," she told the horse. "After all, you still know apples when you smell them." She pulled out the plastic sandwich bags of apple slices she'd brought for him from home and fed him the treat piece by piece. But despite her cheerful words, she couldn't help feeling worried about Pepper. Whatever it was that was wrong with him, he didn't seem to be getting better very quickly.

Lisa heard footsteps in the corridor outside the stall. She looked out and saw Judy Barker approaching. "Hi, Lisa," the vet said when she saw her in Pepper's stall. "How's the old boy doing today?"

"Not very well," Lisa said, trying to keep the anxiety she felt from creeping into her voice. "He seems really tired, and he's sort of puffing and panting as he breathes."

"Hmmm," Judy said. She let herself into the stall with Lisa and greeted Pepper with a pat on the rump. "I'd better have a look."

"What do you think is wrong with him this time?" Lisa asked. "I mean, if this was just a cold or something, he'd be getting better by now, wouldn't he?"

Judy shook her head as she examined Pepper. Lisa could see that the woman's brows were knit. "It doesn't look too good for Pepper, Lisa."

"What do you mean?" Lisa looked from Judy to Pepper and back again. "What's wrong with him?"

"The only thing wrong with him is that he's old. He's had a very full life," Judy said gently. "Lisa, Pepper is dying."

"What?" Lisa couldn't believe she'd heard her correctly. "That's not possible! I mean, I know he's getting older, and that's why nobody rides him anymore, but he's not old enough to *die*!" Lisa's logical mind searched for evidence to back up what she knew in her heart had to be true. "After all, Patch and Nero are both older than Pepper, and nobody's talking about either one of them dying yet."

"Well, that's true," Judy said slowly. "But every horse is different, Lisa, you know that. Nero and Patch both have a lot of quarter-horse blood in them, which may be part of the reason they're still active. But really, it doesn't do any good to compare Pepper to other horses. We just have to look at him as an individual and realize that he's getting too worn-out to go on much longer."

"But there must be something you can do. . . ." Lisa stopped when she saw that Judy was shaking her head again.

"I'm afraid not," the vet said. "We've all got to go sometime, and I'm afraid it's just about that time for dear old Pepper. The best I can do is make him as comfortable as possible for the time being." She paused. "In fact, Max and I have already discussed the possibility of euthanizing him."

Lisa was a straight-A student, and she knew exactly what that word meant. "Euth . . . you mean *killing* him?" she exclaimed, shocked. She felt tears spring to her eyes as she threw her arms around the horse. "No! There must be something else you can do to save him!" She buried her face in Pepper's neck. "He can live longer. Lots of horses have."

Judy touched Lisa's shoulder gently. "I'm sorry, Lisa. I

shouldn't have surprised you with the news this way. Since you spend so much time with Pepper, I thought you must have had some idea. . . ." She let the words trail off.

Lisa's mind felt numb. She couldn't imagine what Pine Hollow would be like without Pepper. Even though she hadn't ridden him in a while, she was used to having him around. It just wasn't possible that she was going to lose him so soon. Judy must be wrong; that was all there was to it. As soon as Max got back, Lisa would insist that he call another vet to get a second opinion.

"Lisa," Judy said, breaking into her thoughts. "I'm sorry. But don't worry. We don't need to be in a hurry about anything. As long as Pepper isn't in serious pain, we can let him be."

The vet stepped back out into the corridor where she had left her medical bag. Lisa loosened her hold on Pepper's neck and wiped her eyes with her hand. The horse snuffled at her face with his soft nose, as if wondering why she was crying.

When she felt a little calmer, Lisa stepped out of the stall after Judy. The vet was scribbling something on a small piece of paper. "Here you go," she said, finishing and handing it to Lisa. "The best thing you can do for Pepper right now is to keep a close eye on him and administer one dose of this medicine whenever he seems uncomfortable. Come on back in the stall with me, and I'll show you how. I've also written down the directions for you in case you forget, and of course you can call me anytime if you have questions."

Lisa paid close attention as Judy explained how much and how often Pepper could be medicated. The vet showed Lisa how to use the syringe, which looked like a giant eye dropper, to put the liquid medicine into the back of Pepper's mouth so that he would have no choice but to swallow it. Then the vet packed up her bag again and headed for the entrance. Lisa trailed along behind her, holding the syringe and the vial of medicine in one hand and the paper containing the instructions in the other.

"I'll call Max and tell him what we're doing," Judy said. She gave Lisa an encouraging smile. "I'm sure he'll be glad to hear that you're helping to take care of Pepper. The old boy couldn't ask for a better nurse."

Lisa managed a small smile in return, although she wished Judy would stop calling Pepper "old." "Thanks. I'll do my best."

The vet said good-bye and hurried out to her truck. Lisa watched as she drove away. Then she went back inside and stood indecisively in the entryway, debating whether or not she should find Stevie and tell her what Judy had said. She decided to check on Pepper again first, so she headed back down the long, deserted corridor to his stall.

"Hi, boy, it's me again," Lisa said softly. The old horse's ears perked up, and he nickered. "That's right," she exclaimed, delighted to see that Pepper seemed to be feeling much better already. "That medicine must be working," she told him.

She scratched him behind the ears and stroked his smooth cheek. His breathing was still heavier than normal, and his head was still hanging a bit low, but other than that he looked much better. Lisa checked him over carefully.

"There's nothing really wrong with you, is there?" she whispered to him. "I'm glad I didn't tell Stevie or Carole about all this after all. They'd just worry, and I know you're really not as sick as Judy thinks you are. I don't need anyone else to tell me that—my own two eyes are enough. No matter what anybody says, I know you'll be fine. I'll help you get better all by myself, Pepper. I promise."

He nuzzled her neck, then let his head drop again, half closing his eyes. She stayed with him for a long time, stroking him and whispering words of encouragement.

CAROLE WAS AWAKENED on Thanksgiving morning by the sound of voices. She recognized the deeper voice as her father's. Sitting up groggily, she wondered who could possibly be out in the hall talking to him so early in the morning.

Suddenly she remembered who: Veronica. For a second Carole considered pulling the covers over her head and going back to sleep, preferably for the whole weekend. But instead, she got up and started gathering her things together to take a shower. After all, she reasoned, it wouldn't be very selfless of her to dump Veronica on her father all day.

Besides that, she had to admit that Veronica really hadn't been much trouble so far. The evening before, Colonel Hanson had taken them out for pizza and a movie. He and Veronica had spent a lot of time talking about their foreign travels, including a lot of places Carole had never even heard of, much less visited. Colonel Hanson's military career had required the family to move frequently when Carole was younger. She had lived on or near military bases all over the country. But though her parents had traveled all over the world before she was born, Carole had never been out of the United States.

Veronica, on the other hand, had been just about everywhere. Carole figured that was just another of the advantages of having wealthy parents. What's more, it seemed to Carole that when her father and Veronica were discussing foreign travel, even on the rare occasions when one or the other of them hadn't actually visited a place, they both still seemed to know an awful lot about it.

Now, as she tried to wake up, she could hear that the two of them were discussing the benefits and drawbacks of someplace called Abu Dhabi. Carole shook her head and laughed. "At least they're getting along," she told her black cat, Snowball. But Snowball just purred and stretched in reply.

By the time Carole had showered and dressed and arrived downstairs, her father and Veronica had already finished breakfast.

"Morning, sleepyhead." Her father greeted her with a kiss on the top of the head. "Happy Thanksgiving!"

"Happy Thanksgiving, Carole," echoed Veronica with a smile.

"Happy Thanksgiving to both of you," Carole replied.

"Grab some cereal, honey, and then you can help us stuff the turkey," Colonel Hanson said.

Carole noticed that Veronica was wearing an apron and holding a dish towel. She stifled a giggle. She was certain that Veronica had never even gone near either object before in her life. But she had to admit that her guest seemed happy enough to be using them now.

Carole gulped down a bowl of cornflakes and joined Veronica at the counter. Colonel Hanson soon had both girls laughing and groaning at his terrible jokes, most of which had a turkey theme in honor of the holiday. Carole was having a lot of fun, and she could tell that Veronica was, too. She was beginning to be glad that she'd invited her.

When they had finished stuffing the turkey, they put it in the oven. "Good job, assistant chefs," Colonel Hanson told them, giving them a mock salute.

They saluted back. "Thanks, Colonel," Carole said. "What next?"

"It's almost time for church," he replied. "Let's get cleaned up."

"Church?" Veronica repeated, seeming confused. "But it's not even Sunday or anything."

"We always go on Thanksgiving," Carole explained to

her. "It's an interdenominational service." She wondered if Veronica would refuse to go.

But Veronica only shrugged. "What should I wear?" she asked.

AFTER THE SERVICE they checked on the turkey, which seemed to be coming along nicely. "Well, there's not really much more to be done right now," Colonel Hanson said. "The turkey should be ready by two, so we can eat then. We can wait awhile before we start getting the other stuff ready."

"So what should we do in the meantime?" Carole asked. *"Miracle on 34th Street* doesn't start for more than an hour."

"Let's see," her father said. He wandered into the living room and opened the cabinet where the Hansons' board games were kept. "How about a game of Monopoly?"

Veronica had followed him and was peering over his shoulder at the stacks of games. "Oh, what a beautiful chess board," she exclaimed, pointing to a board that was leaning against the side of the cabinet by itself. The different-colored squares were formed by dark and light woods.

"Why, thank you, Veronica," said Colonel Hanson proudly. "That board was a gift from my uncle for my high-school graduation."

"Yeah, it's his most prized possession," Carole added with a smile, rolling her eyes.

"I can see why," Veronica said, pulling the board out carefully. "What do the pieces look like?"

Colonel Hanson needed no further urging. He pulled out the case that contained the hand-carved pieces. Setting it on the coffee table, he opened it with a flourish.

Veronica pulled out a piece and examined it. "Beautiful," she said again.

Carole leaned over and selected a piece shaped like a horse's head. "That castle thingy you have is nice, Veronica. But the horse-shaped pieces have always been my favorites."

Colonel Hanson laughed. "That's right. Those are the only pieces I've ever been able to get Carole to show any interest in at all." He put his arm around her shoulders.

Veronica smiled. "Actually, Carole, that horse-shaped piece is called a knight." She held up the piece in her own hand. "And this one that looks like a castle tower is called a rook."

Colonel Hanson's face lit up. "Veronica, do you play?"

Carole groaned. "If you know what's good for you, Veronica, you'll say no. If my dad thinks you're a chess player, he won't leave you alone until you play a game with him."

Veronica laughed. "That's all right. I'd love to play." She winked at Carole. "I should warn you, though, Colonel Hanson, you'd better prepare to lose. My father hasn't been able to beat me in years."

"Aha, a challenge," Colonel Hanson replied. "You're on." Then he looked at Carole. "You don't mind, do you, sweetheart?"

"Oh, I'm sorry, Carole," Veronica added. "Why don't we pick something three can play, instead?"

"No, that's all right," Carole told them both. "Go ahead and play. I don't mind." She didn't, either. She was just glad that her Thanksgiving project was working out so well for everyone. Veronica was obviously having a wonderful time, even though Carole was sure that she still missed her parents. And Carole had to admit that she was having a lot of fun herself. She was sure Veronica would never be one of her best friends—they just didn't have enough in common for that—but now that Carole was getting to know her a little better, she had to admit that Veronica was a lot more interesting than she had thought. And for now, at least, a lot nicer.

As Veronica and Colonel Hanson set up the chess board and began to play, Carole wandered back into the kitchen. She decided to get started on peeling and slicing some of the vegetables for the salad. As she worked, she could hear the chess players from the other room as they kept up a steady stream of joking challenges and insults. Carole smiled proudly. Her father could bring out the best in anybody, she thought as she listened to Veronica laugh. She decided that she could take some of the credit for herself, too, for her generous idea. Maybe Stevie is right about this Thanksgiving stuff after all, Carole thought happily.

THE PHONE RANG at about noon. The chess match had just ended, and just as she had predicted, Veronica had won.

When Carole picked up the phone, Stevie was on the other end. One way that Carole could tell it was Stevie was from the way she just jumped right into the conversation without pausing to identify herself. "Hi, Carole. Listen, can you be at Pine Hollow by four o'clock today? You can bring Veronica if you want. It's very important."

Carole glanced at her father. "Four o'clock? Sure, I guess we'll be finished with dinner by then. What's up?"

"You'll see," Stevie said mysteriously. "Don't be late." She hung up.

Carole shook her head with a smile. She couldn't imagine what Stevie could possibly be up to this time, although she had the funniest feeling that it had something to do with the meaning of Thanksgiving. She and Lisa had long since learned that it was sometimes better not to ask too many questions when Stevie had something up her sleeve. They knew from experience that although her schemes sometimes got them into hot water, they almost always turned out to be a lot of fun.

"What was that all about?" Carole's father asked her as he opened the oven to peek in at the turkey.

"That was Stevie," Carole replied. "She's up to something, but don't ask me what. All she would tell me was to show up at Pine Hollow by four." She noticed that Veronica's face had fallen. "She wants you to come, too, Veronica," Carole added.

"Oh, all right," Veronica said, looking pleased. Carole suspected that she was even happier about being included than she was letting on.

Carole found herself wondering once again what Veronica's life must really be like. It seemed as though her parents weren't interested in spending very much time with her. Maybe that was why Veronica always tried to make people think she was better than everybody else. It could be that her superior attitude was a way of hiding how inferior she felt. Carole thought that was very sad. It was no wonder Veronica didn't seem to have any real friends. All she had was a clique of acquaintances who thought she was perfect and never had any problems.

But if nobody ever knew Veronica had problems, nobody could ever try to help her with them. Carole wondered briefly what *that* would be like, but it was too difficult to imagine. After all, she and her best friends in The Saddle Club were always ready to help each other with any problem they had, whether it was with horses, parents, school, or anything else.

"Come on, Carole, the movie's starting," her father said, interrupting her thoughts. "No popcorn for us today, though. We don't want to spoil our appetites."

Carole followed her father and Veronica into the living room. She had seen *Miracle on 34th Street* many times, and she loved it more every time, but today as she watched, she found her thoughts occasionally returning to Veronica. She was beginning to understand that what Veronica really wanted more than anything was to be included. That was why her parents' leaving her behind had upset her so much. And that was also why she was so glad that Stevie had invited her to come along this afternoon. After all, Carole mused, everyone liked to feel wanted. She was glad she'd had the opportunity to help Veronica. Somehow, despite her earlier fears, Carole thought that Veronica's presence would end up making this year's Thanksgiving extraspecial.

AFTER CALLING CAROLE, Stevie had gone upstairs to find Lisa. She found her in her bedroom. Lisa was rearranging the ribbons she had won since she'd been riding. She'd had them hanging on the bulletin board above her desk, but she had been wondering how they would look on the wall beside her window, so she was holding them up there to see. Since she had won many of the ribbons while riding Pepper, she was also thinking about him. She was just wondering if she should call Red and ask him to check on Pepper, when Stevie burst in.

"Oh, there you are," Stevie exclaimed. "Listen, you've got to meet me at Pine Hollow this afternoon. Be there a little before four."

"This afternoon?" Lisa repeated. "But it's Thanksgiving!"

"I know that," Stevie replied, rolling her eyes. "That's the whole point. Now, look, I have to get going. Just promise me you'll be there, okay?"

"But, Stevie," Lisa said, "you can't go now! We're going to be eating soon."

Stevie shook her head. "Sorry. I can't be there. It's all right, though, I cleared it with your parents."

"Cleared what?" Lisa was used to being confused around Stevie. Most people who spent any time with her at all spent a lot of that time being confused. And it was a good thing Lisa was used to it, because she was definitely confused right now. "Where are you going?"

"Pine Hollow," Stevie told her, a bit impatiently. "I told Red he could take the whole day off to be with his family. I have a ton of stuff to do."

"You mean you told him you'd do all the work yourself?" Lisa said. "Are you crazy? You'll never be able to do it. Besides, you can't skip Thanksgiving dinner!"

"I have to, Lisa," Stevie said. "The horses need me. Thanksgiving is all about sacrifice and generosity, remember? Besides, I've got things to get ready."

"Get ready for what?" Lisa asked, instantly suspicious. "What are you up to?" She could always tell when Stevie was keeping something from her. And she knew that when that happened, it usually meant that Stevie was up to one of her schemes.

"You'll see," Stevie said. "But right now I've got to get going. Just promise you'll meet me at four, okay?" Without even waiting for an answer, Stevie dashed out Lisa's bedroom door to the stairs, taking them two at a time.

"Okay, I'll be there," Lisa called out after her. "But only if you promise me one thing in return."

"What is it?" Stevie called back from halfway down the stairs.

"Check on Pepper for me," Lisa said, hurrying out to the head of the stairs. "Make sure he's feeling okay."

"Will do," Stevie shouted as she disappeared through the Atwoods' front door.

Lisa sat down on the top step and sighed. She couldn't wait for four o'clock. For one thing, she'd get to find out what Stevie was up to, and if Stevie was running true to form, whatever it was would probably be something fun.

But more important, she'd be able to check on Pepper herself.

A FEW MINUTES later Stevie was on her way to Pine Hollow. Lisa's house was only a fifteen-minute walk from the stable, but today Stevie had to walk a little slower than she usually did. That was partly because the temperature had dropped below freezing again the night before and there were patches of ice everywhere. But it was mostly because she was dragging along her little brother Michael's red wagon, and it was overloaded with a strange variety of things that wouldn't make any sense at all to anyone but Stevie. She had already taken over another such load when she'd gone to do the seven-thirty A.M. feeding that morning.

When she arrived, Stevie left the wagon and its contents by the entrance to the indoor ring. Then she set to work, trying to do her chores as quickly as possible so she could move on to the more interesting task that was ahead of her. When she got to Pepper's stall, she remembered her promise to Lisa and checked him over quickly. He looked a little tired, but seemed fine otherwise. She shrugged and gave him a pat on the nose as she left the stall, wondering what Lisa was so worried about.

Finally, she finished everything and headed for the locker area of the stable. There was a large table there, across from the students' cubbies, and with some effort Stevie managed to drag it to the indoor ring. Then she returned for two of the long benches that stood in front of the cubbies. When she had them set up in the ring on either side of the table, she stepped back and brushed off her hands, looking pleased.

But there was no time to lose if she wanted to be ready by four. She set to work unloading Michael's wagon, placing the contents on the ground beside the things she'd brought over earlier that day. First, though, she lifted off the bright-orange paper tablecloth she'd borrowed from Lisa's mother, and which she had used to cover everything else in the wagon. She spread it on the table, noting with satisfaction that it was just the right size.

When everything was unloaded, she opened the large bag containing the papier-mâché food that her school used every year in their Thanksgiving play. There was a giant turkey, only slightly worn-out in a few spots, along with corn, potatoes, and all kinds of other vegetables. It had taken Stevie some effort to track down where the fake food was and convince the teacher who had it to lend it to her. She had made Stevie promise a dozen times that it would be returned in good condition. The teachers at Stevie's school evidently were aware of the reputation the annual Thanksgiving play had among some of the students, and the woman seemed to be afraid that Stevie had some cruel and unusual punishment in mind for the props. But Stevie had finally convinced her otherwise, and she was glad. She was sure the food would add just the right touch.

Next, Stevie began hanging up the paper streamers and assorted Thanksgiving decorations she'd borrowed from her own house and from the Atwoods'. However, she was careful to hang them only in spots where no horse could possibly reach them. The last thing in the world she wanted to have to do was try to explain to Max how one of his horses had gotten a stomachache by swallowing a cardboard pilgrim.

After the ring was festively decorated to her satisfaction, Stevie opened a second bag, smaller than the first. This one contained the paper plates and bowls that she had bought the day before at the dime store in town.

She put some empty plates on the table. Then she filled the rest of the plates and a few of the bowls with the papier-mâché food and set them on the table as well.

"That's the Pilgrims' food," Stevie told one of the stable cats, a gray-and-white tomcat named Seabiscuit, who had wandered into the ring behind Stevie and was now watching her with interest. "The other bowls are the Indians' baskets."

The cat yawned and strolled away. But Stevie didn't even notice, because Lisa, Carole, and Veronica had just arrived. In her excitement Stevie had forgotten that Veronica was coming, and for a second she felt annoyed. She wanted this to be a real Saddle Club project.

Then she reminded herself that the purpose of this project was to spread Thanksgiving spirit. So, in the spirit of Thanksgiving, Stevie decided to accept Veronica's presence cheerfully, just as the Native Americans had accepted the Pilgrims' intrusion on their lands. She definitely felt much better about Veronica's presence when she thought about it that way.

"Hi, you guys," she greeted them all. "You're just in time. I have jobs for all of you. But we have to hurry. Dinner will be served promptly at four."

"Dinner?" said Carole and Lisa in a single voice. Then they groaned. They had both eaten so much at their families' Thanksgiving dinners that they didn't think they'd ever want to so much as look at food again in their whole lives.

Stevie ignored their groans. "Lisa, Veronica, you guys go and get all the horses and tie them in a circle around the table," she said. "Carole, you can help me fill these baskets with apples and oats."

"Baskets?" Carole repeated, staring in confusion at the pile of paper bowls in Stevie's hand.

"Stevie, when are you going to fill us in on what's going on here?" demanded Lisa.

"Isn't it obvious?" Stevie exclaimed. "We're going to put on a Thanksgiving play for the horses!"

"WE'RE *WHAT*?" CAROLE couldn't believe she'd heard Stevie correctly. "Did you say we're putting on a play for the *horses*?"

"Right," Stevie said with a grin.

"But I thought you hated Thanksgiving plays," Lisa said.

"No, no. That's what I was trying to explain before. It's not the plays themselves that I hate," Stevie said. "I guess it's people's reactions that I hate, like when they think that just sitting back and watching a play means they've celebrated the spirit of the whole holiday. But this play is going to be different, because we'll be *in* it, not just watching it."

"I don't get it," Carole said flatly.

But a look of comprehension was dawning on Lisa's

face. "I think I do," she said slowly. "We'll be doing something nice for the horses, by giving them a special feast. And by doing the play—which they won't understand, though they might think it's interesting—we'll also really be doing it for ourselves, to remind ourselves what the whole holiday is really about. Am I close?"

"Bingo," Stevie replied, looking pleased. "I also figured that using the props from my school's stupid play would be a nice touch."

"I thought that fake turkey looked familiar," Veronica said. "Now I know why. I have to stare at it every year through that whole stupid, boring play."

"Right," Stevie said with another grin. "Now, come on, let's get started!"

Despite their initial skepticism, the other girls soon found themselves getting caught up in what they were doing. Stevie's enthusiasm was catching.

As Stevie had directed, Lisa and Veronica brought the horses into the ring and tied their lead ropes to the table or the benches. Soon almost every horse in the stable was standing patiently in a wide circle. The only horse they left in his stall was Geronimo, the stallion. "Sorry, big boy," Lisa said to him, stopping by his stall to pat his nose. She felt bad that Geronimo would miss all the festivities, but she knew better than to take chances by bringing him to the Thanksgiving play. Stallions were much too unpredictable to be safe in such a situation. If he got overexcited, he could hurt himself or someone else.

Lisa wasn't sure that it was a good idea to subject Pepper to all the excitement Stevie had planned either, but when she went to his stall to check on him, he seemed so happy to see her that she couldn't bear to let him miss out on the fun.

In the meantime Stevie and Carole had filled all of the bowls with oats and apples and set them on the table. "All right," Carole said when everything was ready. She stepped back and brushed off her hands on her jeans. "Now what?"

"Are all the horses here?" Stevie asked. She glanced around the ring. "Yep," she said in answer to her own question. She was pleasantly surprised to see that Veronica had brought Garnet out with the others. She hadn't really been sure that the snobby girl would want anything to do with her scheme.

"All present and accounted for," Lisa said.

"Good," Stevie said. "All right, then. Lisa, you and Veronica can be the Pilgrims." She grabbed the bushel barrel that had until recently contained the oats that were now in bowls on the table. "This is Plymouth Rock."

Lisa thought she saw Veronica roll her eyes, but the wealthy girl didn't complain. The two of them stepped up onto "Plymouth Rock" as Stevie had directed, and

Lisa, thinking quickly, even came up with a little speech to begin the play.

"As we Pilgrims land here in the New World," she declared in a very dramatic tone of voice, placing one hand on her chest, "we are determined to live in freedom, free from oppression, free from persecution . . ."

"Free from fifty-cent words like 'persecution,' " Carole heckled from the sidelines.

"Free from people who don't study their vocabulary lessons," Lisa continued, shooting Carole a dirty look as Stevie and Veronica giggled. "Here we will live in peace, with our trusty horses as companions. They will live in peace with the native American horses, just as we will live in peace and brotherhood—I mean sisterhood—with the native American people we find here. . . ."

"There's really no such thing as native American horses, you know," Carole said to Stevie as Lisa continued her silly speech.

"What do you mean?" Stevie asked, looking surprised. "You always see the Native Americans riding horses in those old cowboys-and-Indians movies your father likes so much."

Carole nodded. "They had horses then. But they weren't really native to this country. They came over with the Spanish conquistadors. When the native people first saw the Spanish explorers riding on horseback, they were really scared. They had never seen anything like it, so they thought it must be some new kind of half-human creature."

"Really?" Stevie tried to imagine what someone who had never seen a horse before would think of one, but she couldn't picture it. "It figures you would know something like that," she told Carole. Carole knew more horse facts, obscure and otherwise, than Stevie could learn in a lifetime. And, as her friends liked to tease her, she was ready to share them with everyone at the drop of a hat.

"Hey, what's going on over there?" Lisa demanded from her position on the basket. "Aren't you listening to my inspiring speech?"

"Sorry," Stevie and Carole chorused, doing their very best to sound contrite.

"Well, that's okay," Lisa conceded. "I was just wrapping it up anyway." She cleared her throat and dramatically concluded, "And so I hereby declare that we will work in harmony with all the people here, and do stuff together, and be thankful, and all that kind of thing." She concluded with a little bow, and stepped down off the basket.

"I think it kind of lost something there at the end," Carole commented.

But Stevie had already moved on to the next part of the play. "Now you Pilgrims should build houses and plant food and stuff," she directed Lisa and Veronica.

The two girls exchanged a glance and a shrug and began to pantomime the activities Stevie had suggested.

"What about us?" Carole asked Stevie. "Don't we get to do anything?"

"Of course. I was just getting to that," Stevie said. "We get to be the Native Americans."

"Cool," Carole commented with a grin. "Okay, Pilgrims, here we come!" She and Stevie joined the other two in their playacting, all of them making up the script to their "play" as they went along.

"Look, the horses are watching us," Stevie commented. Sure enough, all of the horses seemed to be observing them closely.

"I hate to disappoint you, Stevie, but I'm afraid it's not your acting ability," Veronica said. "They just smell the apples and oats."

Stevie grinned, not even minding for once that Veronica had sort of insulted her. The snobby girl had actually made a joke!

The girls finished their play, stressing the generosity and cooperation exchanged between the Pilgrims and the Native Americans who had helped them survive in the New World. "Okay, time for the feast," Stevie declared at last.

The girls hurried over to the table and started passing out the treats to the horses, who accepted them eagerly. "Look, Topside has the Thanksgiving spirit," Stevie said. The others turned to see the big bay gelding bobbing his head as he took the pieces of apple Stevie was offering him. "See? He's saying thank you!"

The others laughed, but they had to admit that it did seem that way. After all the food was gone, Lisa made another little speech about all the things the Pilgrims had had to be thankful for, and how good it was for people today to take time out not only to be thankful but to think of ways they could help others.

When she had finished, Stevie clapped enthusiastically. "That's exactly what I was trying to say with this play," she told Lisa. "Thank you for saying it better than I ever could."

"Well, thank you for inviting me to be a part of this," Lisa replied graciously.

"And thank you all for all your help setting it up and everything," Stevie said.

"Let me guess," Carole put in. "Now you're going to thank us in advance for helping you clean up this mess."

Stevie grinned. "You know me too well. And I'm thankful for that." She grabbed the fake turkey from the table and shoved it back into the bag it had come in.

As Stevie finished loading the rest of the fake food into the cart, the other girls all pitched in to help lead the horses back to their stalls. Veronica took Garnet's lead rope and headed out of the ring.

Lisa was standing closest to Topside, so she turned and began to unfasten his lead from the table. She was smiling, thinking about Stevie's unusual play, although she was also wondering if she'd ever come up with a Thanksgiving project of her own. After all, with the play and the job at the stable, Stevie had *two* projects already.

Topside's rope had gotten a little tangled as he moved his head, so it took Lisa a moment to undo it. By the time she and Topside were ready to go, Lisa saw that Carole had taken Pepper's halter and started to lead him out of the ring. But she had stopped and stepped back to look at him. Lisa could see that her friend's forehead was wrinkled with concern.

"Lisa," Carole called, "have you noticed how uncomfortable Pepper seems? He doesn't look well at all."

Lisa nodded. "I've noticed," she said shortly.

Carole and Stevie both turned to stare at her, surprised by Lisa's harsh tone of voice.

"Sorry," Lisa apologized immediately, looking down at Topside's lead rope in her hand. "I didn't mean to snap at you."

"That's all right," Carole said, coming over to Lisa and putting her arm around her shoulders. "But what's wrong with Pepper? How long has he been like this?"

"At least since that night we brought him in from the pasture last week," Lisa told them.

"So that's why you asked me to check on him today," Stevie said. "Has Judy been to see him? Does she know what's wrong with him?"

Lisa nodded. "She's seen him," she said, so quietly that her voice was almost inaudible.

"And?" Stevie said expectantly.

"She said Pepper is . . . dying," Lisa replied, looking up to meet her friends' worried gazes.

"Oh, no!" Carole and Stevie gasped in one voice. "How awful," Carole whispered. "Poor Pepper." She hurried over to hug the old gray horse, who was still standing patiently by the entrance to the ring.

"There must be something Judy can do," Stevie argued. "Hasn't she given him any medicine or anything?"

Lisa nodded and reached into her pocket. "She gave me this to give to him whenever he seems to be in pain." She showed the other girls the medicine.

"Well, I think he definitely needs some now," Carole said. "Let's take him back to his stall. We can give him some of the medicine after we put the rest of the horses away."

The others just nodded without saying anything further, since Veronica had just returned from Garnet's stall. Even though she had been so nice lately, they still knew without discussing it that they didn't want her to know about Pepper. That was something that should remain within The Saddle Club.

"Hey, what are you all doing?" Veronica demanded. "I hope you're not expecting me to put all these horses away myself."

"No, no," Stevie answered quickly. "We're helping." She grabbed Delilah's halter and led the docile mare toward the door. Carole followed with Pepper, and Lisa with Topside.

Soon all of the horses were back in their stalls. Stevie had been trying to come up with a plan to get rid of Veronica while The Saddle Club took care of Pepper, but she needn't have worried. Veronica announced that she wanted to give Garnet a bath before they left and strolled off toward her horse's stall.

Carole shook her head and stared after her. "She's trying. I really think she's trying."

"Well, maybe," Stevie said, sounding a bit skeptical. "But, really, what would she have said if you'd insisted on leaving right now? I mean, she didn't even ask."

Carole shrugged. "It doesn't matter. As long as she's taking care of her horse, I don't mind waiting."

Stevie grinned. She should have expected that response. Carole's first concern was always for the horses' well-being.

"Come on," Lisa urged them. "Let's go see Pepper."

Remembering their mission, The Saddle Club hurried to Pepper's stall. The old horse was again standing facing the back corner, his head hanging low. But Lisa noticed that his breathing didn't seem quite as labored as it had for the last couple of days.

She mentioned this to her friends. "Good," Stevie said. "That must mean that the medicine is working and he's getting better."

"I hope so," Carole said, although Lisa thought she

didn't sound quite as certain as Stevie did. "Anyway, I think we can give him another dose now."

"Okay, let's do it," Stevie said briskly. "Pepper, you'll be better in no time, now that the world-famous Saddle Club medical team is on your case."

Lisa found herself smiling despite her worry. Things really didn't seem so gloomy now that she'd told her friends about Pepper. She wished now that she had confided in them earlier. She should have known they'd see things the same way she did. And she knew that if anybody could help Pepper, it was The Saddle Club. They'd solved lots of seemingly hopeless problems before.

Lisa administered Pepper's medicine, and then all three girls stayed with him for a while. As they petted him and talked to him, he seemed to perk up.

"Either his medicine is working, or he's just enjoying all this attention," Carole said as Pepper lifted his head to nuzzle her curly black hair.

"Probably both," Stevie decided. "See, that proves it. If he keeps taking that medicine for a while, he'll get better. Judy was just being pessimistic. She doesn't realize how brave and strong Pepper really is, and how much he has to live for."

"You're right," Lisa said. And looking at Pepper, she believed that Stevie really could be right. The old horse looked much better than he had a few minutes ago, although he still seemed tired.

"Come on," Carole said, giving Pepper a last pat on

the neck before leaving his stall. "We'd better go help Veronica finish up with Garnet. It's getting late."

Stevie and Lisa said good-bye to Pepper and followed Carole out of the stall. As they walked away, Lisa glanced back to see Pepper's head peering down the corridor after them. Lisa smiled.

LISA AWOKE BEFORE dawn. She knew she had been having a bad dream, and that Pepper had been in it. She didn't recall much else about the dream, except that Pepper had been in trouble and she had been helpless to do anything for him. She couldn't remember any details very clearly. All she knew was that she had been so worried about Pepper that it had made her wake up.

She glanced at the glowing green numbers on her clock radio and groaned. It was much too early even to think about getting up. She rolled over and tried to go back to sleep.

It was no use. She couldn't get Pepper out of her mind. She wasn't sure why she was so worried, since he had seemed to be feeling a little better the day before when she and her friends had been with him. Usually

Lisa was too sensible to let herself be bothered by bad dreams, but there had been something in this one that had scared her more than the monsters and goblins she had sometimes dreamed about when she was younger, although she couldn't quite remember what it was.

She got up and quickly pulled on the jeans and sweater she'd worn the day before, trying not to wake Stevie, who was sound asleep in the other half of the four-poster bed. Even with the heat on, it was chilly in the house at this hour, and the wide wooden floorboards in Lisa's room felt like ice beneath her bare feet. She carefully slid open the top drawer of her dresser and located some warm woolen socks. She put them on, but left her shoes off for the moment so she could walk more quietly.

Lisa managed to find a pen and a piece of paper on her desk without turning on the lights. She quickly scribbled a note to Stevie and set it on her bedside table. In exchange for the note, she picked up the keys to Pine Hollow that Max had given to Stevie and that Stevie had tossed on the bedside table the night before.

Pocketing the keys, along with Pepper's medicine, Lisa wrote another note, this time to her mother. She went downstairs and propped the note on the kitchen table, where Mrs. Atwood would be sure to see it as soon as she came down. Then Lisa put on her shoes and a warm jacket and left the house, pulling the front door closed behind her as silently as she could.

She hurried toward Pine Hollow, her shoes crunching on the frost-hardened grass and her breath forming puffs of steam in the bitterly cold air. She wasn't used to being out at this hour, and as she approached the stable, even the familiar fences and buildings looked strange in the grayish predawn light. Everything was still and silent. There wasn't a soul to be seen anywhere, human or equine. Lisa knew it was because all the horses were stabled inside, but she still thought it gave Pine Hollow a spooky, deserted look, sort of like an Old West ghost town.

"But colder," Lisa whispered to herself with a shiver. She realized that the chill had crept in even through her thick down parka. Wrapping her arms around herself for warmth, she jogged the last few hundred yards to the stable entrance.

She had to take off her gloves to fish the key out of her pocket and fit it into the lock, and her hands grew numb even in the minute it took to do so. She was glad when she heard the click of the lock turning and could slip inside the stable building out of the cold.

Once inside, she wasted no time before heading for Pepper's stall. She didn't even stop to greet the curious horses who looked out and nickered at her as she passed, though she supposed they were probably wondering what she was doing there at this hour.

Lisa had almost grown accustomed to not seeing Pepper's head poking out to greet her as she approached, since these days he seemed to spend most of his time with his head hanging low, facing the back of the stall. She wouldn't have been surprised to see that. But she was surprised by what she did see when she opened the stall door. Pepper was lying on his side in the straw, breathing hard.

"Pepper!" Lisa gasped, going down on her knees and taking his head into her lap. Pepper's eyes looked dull, and his breathing now had a rasping sound to it that Lisa hadn't noticed before. Even though she knew that horses sometimes like to lie down in their stalls for a rest, she also knew that horses as old as Pepper seldom do so, since it's often very difficult for them to get up again. She was afraid that it meant that Pepper had taken a turn for the worse, and she felt the paralyzing sense of worry she remembered from her dream return, stronger than ever. For a second she felt frozen in place, completely helpless to do anything for Pepper, or even to think.

Then her logical mind took over, and she remembered the medicine in her pocket. As she stood up to dig the vial and syringe out of the pocket of her jeans, she noticed for the first time that Pepper hadn't touched the food Stevie had given him the day before. She knew that in a horse a loss of appetite almost always meant trouble.

Lisa carefully measured out a dose of the medication and knelt down again to give it to Pepper. Stroking his cheek, she waited for the medicine to take effect. As she waited, she talked softly to the old horse, not even aware of exactly what she was saying. But that didn't matter. As Max frequently told all the riders at Pine Hollow, horses didn't understand English anyway. But Lisa knew that they did respond to different tones of voice. Now she tried to make her voice as comforting as possible— almost as much for her own benefit as for Pepper's.

As she sat with him, talking all the while, Lisa noticed that Pepper's breathing seemed to get a little bit quieter, although the rasping edge didn't go away. The faithful old horse seemed glad for her company, but Lisa couldn't help noticing that he also seemed less attentive to her than usual. It was as if he were thinking about something else and was just barely aware of her comforting presence. The restlessness she'd noticed in him so often lately was gone, though, and his breathing, while still labored and obviously painful, was slow and steady. His ears, which had once been so alert to every sound around him, flicked toward her occasionally, but like everything else about him, they seemed to be moving almost lazily, in slow motion, as if the effort was just too much for him.

Lisa continued to pet him, and she continued to talk. She realized that she was telling him about how much she had enjoyed every single ride they'd ever had together, from the very first time, at her second riding lesson at Pine Hollow, to the last, on a trail ride just before Pepper's retirement.

"You know, Pepper," she told him seriously, "I think you're one reason I've gotten to love riding so much. I'm sure you've done that for a lot of other people, too. Remember how many people came to see you for your retirement party? They all came to say how much they loved you and appreciated you. And that goes triple for me, you know."

The horse let out a long sigh and blinked. For a second his eyes focused on her; then the faraway look returned as he blinked again more slowly.

"Remember our first horse show?" Lisa asked. "Well, actually, it wasn't really *your* first show, not by a long shot. But it was the first one we were in together, and those ribbons we won showed what a good team we made, didn't they?

"And do you remember when we both got to be in that movie with Skye?" Lisa continued. She and Pepper had both been featured in a movie that had been filmed at Pine Hollow. Skye Ransom, the teenage star of the movie, had asked Lisa to pick out a horse for him to ride. She had chosen Pepper, knowing that the calm and obedient horse would be perfect for the role—especially since Skye wasn't a very good rider. Lisa smiled a little at the memory. Making the movie had been much harder work than she had expected, but it had also been a lot of fun. Her smile faded, though, as she realized just how many of her favorite Pine Hollow memories in-volved Pepper. Could things ever be the same without him?

"That was exciting, wasn't it, boy?" she continued, trying to banish such thoughts. She was supposed to be comforting Pepper, not feeling sorry for herself. "And how about that time . . ."

The words tumbled from her mouth faster and faster as more memories flooded her mind. She reminisced about all the good times she and Pepper had had to-gether, telling him over and over again how much she had appreciated every single moment of it all. She talked about the Mountain Trail Overnight they'd gone on to-gether, and the magical Starlight Ride they'd shared on Christmas Eve. She reminded him how much fun it had been to learn to play polocrosse together. Then, of course, there was that very first show—a combined-training event at Pine Hollow at which Lisa and Pepper had won three ribbons. There was so much to remember that Lisa didn't think she could ever finish telling Pep-per about how much fun it had all been. And she didn't want to.

As she talked, Lisa looked as hard as she could for signs that the medicine was working. But aside from qui-eting his breathing a little, she had to admit that it didn't seem to be having much effect. "Pepper, you have to get better," she told him fiercely, straightening his forelock with her fingers. "You just have to!"

But as the horse sighed again and his ears drooped a little, Lisa could tell how much effort it was costing him just to breathe. His eyes closed, and in a few seconds he was asleep.

"It's okay, Pepper," Lisa whispered. "Don't worry. I'm here with you now. Everything's going to be okay."

But as she said it, she realized that she needed to hear those words more than Pepper did. In fact, she realized that he already seemed to know what she herself was just beginning to understand.

"Pepper," she said quietly to the sleeping horse. "You've done so much for me, ever since I've known you, and for everybody else around here, too." She took a deep breath. "And I think I've finally realized what I need to do for you right now. I don't like it much, but I think it's the best thing for *you*, and that's what's important."

She stroked Pepper's cheek again gently, being careful not to wake him. She knew she had to say the words out loud. Otherwise, she'd never be able to carry them through. "Pepper, you're in pain all the time now, and it's not fair to you. You've been too good to me for me to make you go through this any longer than you have to, especially if it's just because of my own selfishness. If it's just because I can't stand to see you die. But it's time now for me to do what's best for you. Stay right here and rest, and I'll go call Judy."

She lifted his head off her lap and lowered it carefully to the straw on the stall floor. Pepper didn't wake up, and he didn't move as she left the stall. She could hear the sound of his rasping breathing following her down the corridor as she walked toward Max's office to use the phone.

Lisa noticed that the sun had risen while she was with Pepper. She was surprised that so much time had passed. Then again, she realized that she had had a lot to talk about with Pepper before she said good-bye.

Lisa called Judy first. The vet promised to be there within the hour. Next, Lisa called her own house. When her mother answered, she quickly explained what was happening and asked to talk to Stevie.

"Hello?" Stevie's voice came groggily over the phone a few minutes later. "Lisa? Where are you?"

"Pine Hollow," Lisa replied. "I came over because I was worried about Pepper. With good reason, as it turns out. Stevie, he's much worse." Lisa's voice cracked a little as she said it.

That seemed to wake Stevie up right away. "How much worse?" she asked.

"A lot," Lisa replied truthfully. Even though Lisa was feeling so bad about Pepper, it felt good to share some of her worry and pain with her friend. "In fact, I just called Judy. She'll be here soon. I think it's time to let Pepper go." For the first time that morning, Lisa felt tears come to her eyes. She choked them back. "I think that's the best thing for him."

"I'll be there as soon as I can," Stevie told her. "Have you talked to Carole yet?"

"N-n-n-" Lisa couldn't quite get the word out, because she was trying so hard to keep from crying.

"I'll call her," Stevie said quickly. "We'll both be there soon. Probably Veronica, too, unfortunately, unless we can manage to lose her somewhere along the way."

Lisa tried to laugh at Stevie's joke, but all she could manage was a sniffle.

"Don't worry, Lisa. Just hold on until we get there," Stevie said comfortingly, realizing that her friend was much too upset for jokes at the moment. Stevie was upset, too, but besides being worried about Pepper, she was worried about Lisa. She knew how much Pepper meant to Lisa, and if he had to be put down, Stevie wanted to be there for both of them.

Stevie said good-bye to Lisa and then immediately dialed Carole's number.

"Veronica and I will be there in a few minutes," Carole said as soon as Stevie told her what was wrong. "I'm sure my dad will drive us. We'll pick you up on the way, okay?"

Meanwhile Lisa had called Red O'Malley and then returned to Pepper's stall to wait for everyone to arrive.

She knew that the most important thing she could do for Pepper now was to stay with him and let him know that she cared, and that he wasn't alone. She had done what she knew was right. Now she just hoped she would be able to handle the consequences.

10

COLONEL HANSON DROPPED off Carole, Stevie, and Veronica in front of Pine Hollow, and the three of them hurried inside. On their way to Pepper's stall, they met Red, who was heading in the same direction.

"How's Pepper?" Carole asked him anxiously.

"And Lisa?" Stevie added.

Red shook his head. "The answer to both questions is 'I don't know.' I just got here myself."

By this time they had reached Pepper's stall, so they didn't waste any more time talking. Stevie and Carole looked in over the half door of the stall and saw Lisa sitting in the straw with Pepper's head in her lap. She was talking to him softly, and he seemed to be listening. His big brown eyes were trained on Lisa's face.

"Lisa, we're here," Stevie said.

Lisa looked up. "Hi. Thanks for coming," she said. "Pepper was sleeping for a while, but he just woke up a few minutes ago."

Carole turned to Red, who had joined them at the door. "He doesn't look too good, does he?" she said quietly.

The stable hand shook his head. "Lisa did the right thing by calling Judy," he said sadly. "Poor old Pepper."

Carole nodded. So did Stevie. They both would have sworn that they heard Veronica, who was hanging back from the door, stifle a sniffle.

Just then they all heard the sound of Judy's truck coming to a stop in front of the stable. A moment later she joined them, holding the black bag containing her medical supplies. She greeted them briefly, asked Stevie to hold the bag, and then entered the stall.

Lisa stood up and stepped back to allow Judy enough space to examine Pepper. But the vet hardly seemed to need it; the examination was brief. Judy gave the horse a pat and then stood up. She faced Lisa, put one hand on her shoulder, and looked at her solemnly.

"Lisa, thank you for having the courage to make the very difficult decision to call me," the vet said quietly. "I want you to know that it was the right decision, even if it doesn't feel that way to you right now. Pepper is very sick, and he's not going to get better. There's no need for him to suffer any longer. Now he won't have to."

Lisa just nodded. She didn't trust herself to speak.

Despite the vet's words, Lisa kept wondering if this was really the only way. But deep inside of herself, she knew that it was.

"You all might prefer not to be here for this," Judy was saying as she reached over the stall door to take her bag from Stevie.

Lisa took a deep breath. "I want to be here," she said. "After all, I've come this far with him."

Stevie nodded quickly. "We all want to stay."

"That's right," Carole said quietly. Lisa wondered briefly if Carole was thinking about her mother's death. If it was this hard for her to lose a horse she loved, she couldn't even imagine what her friend had gone through in losing a parent. She promised herself to think more about that later and then turned her attention back to Pepper.

Lisa knelt down in the hay beside Pepper again. Carole and Stevie joined her. "I guess it's really time to say good-bye to him," Lisa said, looking at her friends.

Carole just nodded. But Stevie grabbed Pepper's big head in her hands and carefully turned it a little so he was looking straight into her face. He blinked at her, seeming surprised to see her.

"Don't give me that look, Pepper," Stevie said, trying her best to sound stern, and failing miserably. "You don't think I'd let you go without a proper good-bye, do you?" And to the amazement of all watching, Stevie planted a big kiss right on the end of Pepper's velvety gray nose.

Then she leaned over and hugged him. "We'll never forget you, Pepper."

Next it was Carole's turn. She stroked Pepper's cheek and spoke to him seriously. "Pepper, you've been a good friend to us all. Before I say good-bye, I want to sing you a special song that my mother used to sing to me at night when I was afraid of the dark and couldn't go to sleep. I hope it'll keep you from being afraid now, too."

Stevie and Lisa glanced at each other. Neither of them had known that Carole had ever been afraid of anything.

But Carole didn't look up. As she continued to stroke Pepper's smooth cheek, she sang a short lullaby in a soft, sweet voice. When she finished, her eyes were filled with tears. She hugged Pepper just as Stevie had done. "You've earned your rest, Pepper. Good-bye."

As Lisa moved forward, Stevie and Carole stood up and stepped back against the wall of the stall. They wanted to give Lisa one last moment alone with Pepper.

Lisa would have appreciated the gesture if she'd noticed it, but at that moment all she could think about was Pepper. She sat down beside him and took his head into her lap one last time. She brushed his forelock out of his eye and patted him on the neck, just as she had always done when she was proud of him or pleased with something he'd done or just showing her affection for him. Now that the moment had come, Lisa found that she had no idea what to say to him. As often as she'd been told that horses couldn't understand English, she still felt it was very important to say the right thing.

But suddenly Lisa understood that she didn't really have to say much at all. She had said it all many times before, and all that was necessary now was a few words to sum it all up. She leaned down, put both arms around Pepper's neck for a farewell hug, and spoke right into one of his big pointed gray ears. "I love you, Pepper," she whispered. "Thank you." Then she kissed him on the forehead and stood up. She stepped to the door of the stall and looked out at Judy, Red, and Veronica. "We're ready," she said, her voice calm and steady.

Judy nodded and stepped back into the stall. She had prepared an injection while The Saddle Club was saying good-bye to Pepper.

"Can we pat him while—while you do it?" Lisa asked.

"Of course," Judy told her. "I'm sure he'd like that."

The three girls knelt down again. Carole was in front of Pepper, where she could stroke his neck, and Stevie was by his back, where she could lay her hand on his side. Lisa sat down by his head, where she could continue to stroke his cheek and comfort him until his pain was gone forever.

Judy crouched down next to Stevie, gave Pepper a fond pat on the neck, and then administered the injection. It worked swiftly. Within a matter of seconds, the girls felt a shudder pass through Pepper's body. He closed his eyes, let out one last sigh, and then lay still.

11

AFTER THEY LEFT Pepper's stall, The Saddle Club wandered toward the locker area, where the riders stored their extra clothing and equipment. Veronica trailed along behind them. For once in her life she didn't seem to have anything to say. Judy had stayed behind to wait for the truck to come and remove Pepper's body. Red had gone to check on the rest of the horses and start the morning feeding, which by this time was late.

Lisa felt drained. It had been a very long morning; so long, in fact, that she could hardly believe it was only nine o'clock. She also could hardly believe that Pepper was really gone. Most of all, though, she could hardly believe that her stomach was growling. Somehow, it didn't seem right to be hungry at a time like this, but her stomach didn't seem to know it.

"Are you all right?" Stevie asked, putting an arm around her shoulders.

Lisa nodded and smiled at her friend. Stevie seemed fun-loving and carefree most of the time, but she was proving right now that there was more to her than that. There was also a caring, sympathetic friend, who knew how much Pepper had meant to Lisa. "Thanks. I think I'm going to be okay," Lisa said. And she meant it. She was sure that later, when what had happened had had a chance to sink in, she would be sad and cry, probably a lot. But she also knew that she had done what was right for Pepper, and that was the most important thing.

Lisa and Stevie sat down together on one of the benches in the locker area. It was hard for Lisa to believe that it had only been the day before that they had used the very same bench in their Thanksgiving play. It felt to her as if years and years had passed since then.

She noticed that Carole and Veronica were standing together nearby. Lisa couldn't hear what they were saying, but she could see that Carole was doing most of the talking. She had a sad and thoughtful look on her face, and Lisa suspected she was talking about Pepper. But after a moment Lisa saw that Veronica had interrupted and leaned forward as if she were asking Carole something important. Lisa couldn't imagine what it was, however, especially when she saw Carole frown with annoyance.

This time Lisa and Stevie could both hear exactly

what their friend was saying. "You know, Veronica, you've been so human lately that I'd almost forgotten how selfish you can be. But you just reminded me!" Carole snapped loudly. Then she turned on her heel and marched away from an astonished Veronica toward Lisa and Stevie.

"What was that all about?" Stevie asked as Carole joined them on the bench.

But before Carole could answer, Veronica strolled over and stopped before them, her hands on her hips. "Well, you guys, this has been very interesting, but I have to go. I have something to do at home."

"Don't let us keep you," Carole said, still looking angry.

Veronica headed for the door. But she paused just before reaching it and turned to look at Lisa. "I'm really sorry about Pepper," she said quietly, then dashed out.

Stevie raised her eyebrows. "I can't believe I'm saying this, but that was nice of her to say." She turned to Carole. "Now will you tell us what she just said to you that obviously *wasn't* so nice?"

"I will," Carole said, "as soon as we get to TD's. I think this day definitely calls for a Saddle Club meeting."

Lisa stared at her. "Carole, I'm pretty upset about Pepper and everything, and I hardly got any sleep at all last night, but even I know it's barely nine o'clock in the morning. Don't tell me you're in the mood for ice cream now!" Tastee Delight, more commonly known as TD's, was an ice-cream parlor at the local shopping center. It was one of The Saddle Club's favorite places to hold their meetings.

"Even if she is, she's out of luck," Stevie announced. "TD's doesn't open until eleven. I know that for a fact, because one time I *was* in the mood for an ice-cream breakfast."

"Oops," Carole said, blushing. "I guess I wasn't thinking. Well, maybe we can go somewhere for breakfast, then. All I know is that I'm starving." Carole was so responsible and knowledgeable when it came to horses that her friends sometimes forgot that she could be a bit flaky in situations where no horses were involved. But Carole invariably found an opportunity to remind them.

Lisa started to laugh, but she could see that Carole was truly embarrassed by her error. She realized that the morning had been difficult for all of them. So instead of laughing, she suggested a solution. "Why don't we take the bus over to that pancake house on the other side of town?" she said.

"Good idea," Carole said, brightening immediately.

"It is a good idea, but I can't go," Stevie said reluctantly. "I have a job to do here, remember?"

Red had entered the area just in time to hear what Stevie said. "Did I hear you correctly, Stevie? You're going to pass up breakfast with your friends to stay here and muck out stalls with me? I'm touched!" he teased, putting one hand over his heart. Then he got serious. "Go on, Stevie. It's been a rough morning, and you probably need a break."

"But I promised Max, and besides, you're running late already . . ." Stevie began.

But Red didn't let her finish. "Don't be ridiculous. Go!" he insisted. Then he hurried out of the room before she could protest further.

Carole, for one, didn't need to hear it twice. "You heard him, Stevie. You've been doing a great job here while Max was away, but you *do* deserve a break. After all, Red owes you one from yesterday, when you took care of everything yourself all day."

Stevie didn't say anything. Instead, she dug her hands into the pockets of her jeans and looked worried.

Carole knew Stevie so well that at certain times, she could almost read her mind. This was one of those times. "Don't worry, Stevie," she said. "I have some extra money you can borrow for bus fare. *And* for breakfast."

"Oh, great," Stevie exclaimed, looking relieved. "So what are we doing still hanging around here? Let's go!"

A SHORT TIME later The Saddle Club was seated in a large booth in the bustling, brightly lit interior of Let Them Eat Pancakes, which was on the opposite side of Willow Creek from Pine Hollow. Before leaving the stable, the girls had called Lisa's parents and asked them to pick them up there in an hour and a half. They knew it wouldn't take nearly that long to eat, but they had a lot to talk about.

The cheerful young waiter handed them each a menu and returned a moment later with three glasses of water. "I'll be back in a few minutes to take your orders," he promised before rushing off to take care of a large table that was occupied by what looked like an entire troop of Cub Scouts.

Stevie raised her eyebrows as she watched him start to take their orders. "I have the funniest feeling we're not going to see that waiter for a while," she predicted.

As they waited, the three girls chatted about the events of the past few days. Carole and Stevie tried to keep the conversation upbeat to take Lisa's mind off Pepper's death. They knew she would talk about it with them when she was ready, but they didn't want to rush her.

"So, Stevie," Carole said, picking up a menu. "What have you learned about the meaning of Thanksgiving this week?"

"A lot, actually," Stevie said. "For one thing, I learned that just when I thought my school's play couldn't possibly get any more boring—it did!"

The others laughed. "At least the other Thanksgiving play you saw this week was much more interesting," Lisa reminded her, thinking again of the play Stevie had masterminded at Pine Hollow. Lisa had thought it was a pretty silly idea at first but had ended up enjoying herself. And it really had made her think about the meaning of the holiday, especially when she was making up her speech.

"Right. And I'll bet the audience was a lot more appreciative," Carole added. "Maybe next year your school should try serving oats and apples after the play."

Stevie grinned. "It was a good idea, wasn't it?" she said. "But anyway, I also learned something a little more important this week."

"That taking care of an entire stable full of horses all by yourself is hard work?" Lisa guessed.

"That papier-mâché turkey doesn't taste as good as the real thing?" Carole teased.

"Even better," Stevie replied. "I learned that it's hard to be totally selfless. Maybe impossible."

Carole wrinkled her brow. "But I thought you were having fun helping out at Pine Hollow this week. I mean, I know it was hard work, but . . ."

"No, no," Stevie said. "That's not exactly what I mean. It's the totally selfless part that's hard, not the generous part. I mean . . ."

"I think I know what you mean, Stevie," Lisa said, coming to her rescue. "You found out that doing something generous makes you feel good, and maybe helps you learn new things, too. So even though your motives might be selfless when you begin, the experience itself doesn't feel selfless at all, since you benefit, too."

Stevie looked at her gratefully. "That's exactly it, Lisa."

"Lisa, sometimes I think you should take on a full-time job as Stevie's interpreter," Carole said with a laugh.

"Oh, I don't know," Lisa said. "You're pretty fluent in Stevie-ese yourself. Remember that incident with the bus fare?"

They all laughed at that, Stevie most of all. But then she quieted down and looked at Lisa seriously. "How are you doing, Lisa?" she asked. "I wish I were as good at Lisa-ese as you are at Stevie-ese, so I'd know what you're thinking about right now."

Carole nodded. "Me, too. We're all sad about Pepper, but you're really the one who was the closest to him."

Lisa shrugged. "I guess I'm okay," she said. "I keep thinking about Pepper, and I feel really sad and sort of empty inside, but I also feel kind of relieved in a strange way, because I know that at least he's not in pain anymore. So I guess I'm upset for me, but kind of, well, happy for him, I guess. Does that sound weird?"

"Not at all," Carole said. "You really did the right thing by deciding it was time to call Judy."

"That's what everybody keeps saying," Lisa said. "But I miss him terribly already. I still can't quite believe he's gone forever."

"Me, neither," said Carole and Stevie in a single voice. They were quiet for a moment. Then Carole spoke. "Actually, Lisa, I think you really did discover the secret to true selflessness."

"I did?" Lisa said.

"She did?" Stevie said at the same time.

Carole nodded. "You did something that was very painful to you. After all, you'll miss Pepper like crazy, probably more than anyone else. And it must have been practically impossible for you to make the decision to let him die."

Lisa nodded, looking down at her hands.

"Well," Carole continued, "but that's only looking at the situation from your point of view. From Pepper's point of view, he was in terrible pain and discomfort most of the time, and it just kept on getting worse and worse. The most important thing was to prevent that from going on any longer than necessary, once it became clear that Pepper wasn't ever going to get better. So what you did was the best thing for him, even though it was hard for you."

Lisa nodded again and looked up at Carole. "You're right. That's why I did it—why I knew I *had* to do it. I guess I just never thought about it as selflessness before." She shrugged. "I've been so busy worrying about Pepper and helping Stevie at the stable that I never had a chance to think of my own Thanksgiving project. But I guess one sort of found me itself, didn't it?"

"Well, I for one am proud of you for being able to do it. I don't know if I could have," Stevie said frankly. She raised her water glass and saluted Lisa with it. "Here's to you."

"Hear! Hear!" Carole agreed wholeheartedly, raising her own glass.

"Thanks," Lisa said, smiling at her two best friends. "And as long as we're making toasts, I have one of my own."

"Go for it," Stevie encouraged her.

Lisa raised her glass. "Here's to Pepper. Long may his memory live and inspire us to be the best riders we can be."

Carole knew that Lisa was thinking about everything Pepper had taught her about riding. She definitely agreed with the sentiment. "Hear! Hear!" she said again. The three girls clinked their glasses together and then they each took a drink.

Lisa was glad she'd made the toast to Pepper, but it had made her feel as though she might start to cry. She decided the safest thing to do was change the subject. "So, Carole," she said as she set her glass down. "I've been so preoccupied lately that I haven't had a chance to find out how things were going with you and Veronica."

"Yeah, talk about selfless," Stevie added. "How is it living with the self-proclaimed queen of Willow Creek? Did she bring any of her servants with her?"

"Or complain because you didn't have any pure-silk sheets for her to sleep on?" Lisa joked.

"Or borrow any twenty-dollar bills from your father to blow her nose on?" Stevie added.

"Enough, enough!" Carole exclaimed, laughing. "The answer to all of those things is no. Veronica was practically the perfect guest. She and my dad got along famously. It turns out they're both travel buffs, not to mention chess freaks. She even beat him at a game."

Stevie cocked an eyebrow. "It almost sounds like it was fun having her there."

Carole shrugged. "You know, I would have preferred spending the time alone with Dad, but it wasn't as bad as I was afraid it was going to be, and as rotten as Veronica is most of the time, I was happy to see that even she has a nice side. It made me glad I invited her. And I guess it really proves there's good in everyone."

"I noticed she's been awfully nice lately," Lisa said.

"I noticed, too," Stevie said. "I couldn't believe it, but I noticed it. I wonder what's gotten into her?"

"Well, unfortunately, whatever it was, I think it's gotten *out* of her again," Carole said. "You'll never believe what she said to me back at Pine Hollow after Pepper died."

"What?" Stevie asked curiously. She had almost forgotten about the strange exchange she and Lisa had witnessed in the locker area.

Carole shook her head in disgust. "She said she hoped that now Max would let her put Garnet in Pepper's stall."

"Why?" Lisa asked, confused.

"Isn't it obvious?" Carole said. "Not only is Pepper's stall bigger than Garnet's, it's also closer to the tack room. Now, on the infrequent occasions when Veronica tacks or untacks Garnet herself—"

"Better make that *extremely* infrequent," Stevie interrupted.

"Okay," Carole continued, "on the *extremely* infrequent occasions when Veronica tacks or untacks Garnet herself, she won't have as far to walk to the tack room." It was true. The stall Pepper had spent his last days in was only a few yards from the tack room. It actually wasn't his original stall, because a horse named Prancer was living there now. But it was one that had been empty when Pepper had moved back inside, and it was large and spacious, not to mention well located.

At first all three of them felt angry at Veronica for being so selfish. But then, as she realized how ridiculous the whole thing was, Lisa began to giggle. As she did, she felt some of the tension she'd been feeling about Pepper drift away. She still felt an aching sadness that she knew wouldn't go away anytime soon, but even that couldn't stop the laughter from bubbling out of her.

At first Stevie and Carole looked surprised, but soon they were giggling, too. "Whew," Carole said when they had quieted down again. "It feels good to laugh."

To her surprise Lisa found herself agreeing. "But I do think it's kind of sad that Veronica is so selfish. Even

Pepper's death didn't make her stop thinking of herself for very long."

"I know," Carole said thoughtfully. "I really do feel kind of sorry for her. I think she's had a pretty lonely life. She wants to belong, but she never really learned how, and now she's so obnoxious that nobody wants to help her learn."

"Lonely?" Stevie said. "Come on. She's always had all that money to keep her company. And she never lets us forget it."

Carole shrugged. "Still, I know I'd rather have my life than hers. That's one thing I've spent a lot of time thinking about for the past few days. Veronica may have a ton of money and trips around the world and her own purebred Arabian mare, but I wouldn't trade my friends and family for all that." She paused for a moment to consider what she'd just said. "Although," she added, "I wouldn't mind having Garnet myself."

Lisa and Stevie laughed. "Don't let Starlight hear you say that," Stevie teased. "He'd be jealous."

"Starlight will always come first with me, you know that," Carole replied quickly. Then she laughed. "But where is it written that I can have only *one* horse?"

"Well, in your father's checkbook, for one," Stevie said. She ducked just in time to avoid the spray of water that Carole had just flicked at her from her glass.

"Speaking of jealousy, which reminds me of romance . . ." Lisa began, realizing that there was something else she'd been forgetting to think much about lately. Her friends were instantly all ears.

"Are you referring to that romantic fellow, Max Regnery?" Stevie guessed with a sly grin.

Lisa nodded. "I wonder how his weekend is going with his mystery woman."

"I hope he's having a good time," Carole said.

"I hope we get to meet her," Lisa said.

"I hope all that stuff, too," Stevie said. "But right now, I mostly hope that waiter gets over here to take our order soon. I'm starving!"

As if he'd heard her, the waiter appeared at their table at that very moment. "Sorry to keep you waiting, ladies," he said breathlessly. "Can I take your order?"

Stevie noticed that the waiter was pretty young, maybe college-age, and very cute. In fact, he reminded her a little bit of her boyfriend, Phil. Because of that, she almost felt bad about what she was about to do to him. Almost.

Lisa was already ordering. "I'll have the banana pancakes with maple syrup," she told the waiter.

"And you?" he asked, turning to Carole.

"I think I'll try the French toast," she decided. "And a glass of orange juice, please."

The waiter turned to Stevie. "And for you, miss?" he asked, his pen poised expectantly over his notepad.

Stevie gave him a devilish grin. "Well, I'm pretty hungry . . ." she began.

"Uh-oh," Carole whispered to Lisa. Stevie was famous for the bizarre and frequently revolting combinations of ice cream and toppings she always ordered at TD's, and Carole and Lisa had a feeling they knew what was coming.

And they were right. ". . . so I'd like the half-dozen flapjack special," Stevie continued sweetly.

"Gotcha," the waiter said cheerfully, jotting a note on his pad.

"Wait, I'm not finished," Stevie said as the young man started to turn away. "I'd like to make a couple of adjustments to the special."

"No problem," the waiter said. "What would you like?"

"First of all," Stevie said briskly, "I'd like two of those pancakes to be blueberry, two to be buckwheat, and the other two to be raisin-walnut. Then, on top of them all, I'd like some honey, some boysenberry syrup, some peach jam, and some mint sauce. Oh, and do you happen to have any chocolate syrup?"

The waiter nodded weakly.

"Good. Add a double portion of that. Oh, and maple syrup, too, of course, and some fresh strawberries."

"Of course," the waiter said with a gulp, writing it down. "Will—will that be all?"

"Well, let's see," Stevie mused. "Do you have any maraschino cherries, by any chance?"

"Uh, I'll have to check with the kitchen," the waiter

said, rushing away before Stevie had the chance to say another word.

"That wasn't very nice of you, Stevie," said Lisa, trying to keep from smiling. "Where's your Thanksgiving spirit?"

"That poor guy probably thought those Cub Scouts were going to be his toughest customers of the day," Carole said, shaking her head. "He didn't even see it coming. At least the waitress at TD's knows what to expect. More or less." The regular waitress at TD's had heard Stevie order so many of her crazy concoctions that she paled as soon as she saw The Saddle Club enter the ice-cream parlor.

Stevie just grinned again. "And my brothers are always telling me that men have stronger stomachs than women," she commented. "I think we've just proved them wrong. Isn't that wonderful?"

And in spite of themselves, Carole and Lisa had to admit that it was.

12

THE NEXT DAY, much to Carole's relief, the diAngelos returned from the Bahamas and Veronica went home. Veronica had returned to being nice after the incident about Pepper's stall, but Carole was glad that her life would now be able to return to normal. Veronica hadn't really demanded caviar for breakfast and daily massages as Stevie still seemed to suspect, but her presence had meant some life-style changes for Carole, who was used to being an only child and not having to share her father with anyone.

When she told her father what she was thinking after Veronica left, he gave her a hug and told her he was glad he didn't have to share her anymore, either. He also said that he was proud of her for inviting Veronica to share their Thanksgiving. It was quite obvious to him that

Veronica's home life was far from perfect, and he just hoped that being with them had helped her a little. Carole agreed, thinking—not for the first time—that her father was a very wise man. She gave him another big hug for that.

Carole was also glad that she wouldn't have to bring Veronica along with her to Pine Hollow that day. Max and Mrs. Reg were scheduled to return at around three o'clock in the afternoon, and Carole, Stevie, and Lisa had arranged to meet shortly before that time so they could greet them upon their return. For one thing, The Saddle Club wanted to be able to tell Max and Mrs. Reg about Pepper in person. For another thing, The Saddle Club wanted to hear all about Max's romantic weekend in person, and meet his girlfriend if he brought her back with him as they were hoping he would.

Carole arrived half an hour early so she'd have enough time to give Starlight a quick grooming before her friends arrived. She'd been so busy lately with Veronica and Thanksgiving and everything else that she hadn't been able to spend as much time as usual with her horse, and she missed him. He seemed to miss her, too, since he nuzzled her as she entered his stall—although that could have been because of the carrots she had in her pocket. Carole didn't believe in spoiling horses with a lot of treats, but this time she felt that Starlight deserved it. Part of the reason was that she hadn't spent enough time with him for the past few days.

But she knew that another part of it was that she wanted to thank him just for being there.

Carole had been so busy worrying about how Lisa was feeling that Pepper's death hadn't really hit her until that morning, when she had arrived at the stable and walked past his empty stall. Even at her young age, Carole felt that she'd already had more than her share of experience with death. Her mother's death from cancer had been the worst thing that had ever happened to Carole. When Cobalt had died, Carole hadn't been sure she could handle that kind of pain again, but somehow, she had.

Since then, working with Judy, Carole had seen other horses die, and she had felt the same kind of painful sadness for every single one of them. No matter how many times it happened, it never got any easier to take. When she had seen Pepper's empty stall, the knowledge that she would never again see his familiar gray face looking out at her over the half door hit her heart like a fist in the stomach. The most comforting thing she could think of to do, luckily, was what she'd been planning to do anyway. She could take care of her own horse, to make sure that his life was as comfortable and happy as she could make it—as comfortable and happy as Pepper's long life had been, thanks to Lisa and Carole and Stevie and Max and Mrs. Reg and Red and a whole list of other people who had loved and cared for him.

As Carole set to work brushing the straw and dust

from Starlight's rich reddish-brown coat, she found herself thinking about Lisa again, and how very different the two of them were from each other in some ways. She remembered how upset she had been after Cobalt had died. Even her friends hadn't been able to make her feel better at first. Although Carole knew that Lisa was very sad about Pepper's death, she seemed to be handling it a lot better than Carole had handled Cobalt's. She had been able to talk and laugh with her friends at breakfast, and in her typically logical way had even begun to sort out and analyze her own feelings about what had happened.

Still, Carole reminded herself, the two situations had been very different. Cobalt's death had been a tragic accident, caused by human carelessness, that had cut his life short while he was still very much in his prime. Carole had never even had a chance to say good-bye to him. Pepper, on the other hand, had simply reached the natural end of a long life. What's more, Lisa had been able to take part in bringing that life to a humane end, and that was something she could feel good about even in her sadness.

The situations were very different, Carole decided, but she and Lisa were very different as well. And that was okay. More than okay, it was what made The Saddle Club such a wonderful group. Each member had different strengths, so that together they were stronger than the sum of their parts.

When Stevie and Lisa arrived shortly before three, they found Carole just finishing Starlight's grooming. "Come on," Lisa said. "If you're finished with Starlight, let's go wait out front."

"All right," Carole said. After giving Starlight a last affectionate pat, she picked up her grooming bucket and let herself out of the stall. She suspected that Lisa was anxious about what she was going to say to Max about Pepper. "I'm finished."

The girls settled down in the locker area, where they could hear the sounds of approaching cars. They didn't have long to wait before they heard one turning into the drive. They hurried outside and spotted Max's car coming to a stop in front of Pine Hollow, pulling the smaller of the stable's two horse vans behind it.

Max and Mrs. Reg barely had time to step out of the car before Stevie started talking at them a mile a minute. She wanted to tell them about everything she'd done as an assistant stable hand.

"Nice to see you, too, Stevie," Max said with a laugh. Carole noticed that he seemed to be in a good mood. She wondered if that meant he'd had a good weekend with his girlfriend. She hoped it did.

Lisa took a deep breath and stepped forward. Stevie stopped talking in midsentence, remembering that Lisa wanted to be the one to tell Max about Pepper. "Oh, here's Lisa," Stevie said awkwardly.

"Hello, Lisa," Max said to her.

"Hi, Max. Hi, Mrs. Reg," Lisa replied automatically. "I wanted to tell you about . . . about Pepper."

Mrs. Reg stepped forward and laid one hand on Lisa's arm. "We know, Lisa. Judy called us."

"I know that," Lisa said. "But I just wanted to say . . ." Then she stopped, as she realized she really didn't know what she wanted to say.

"You don't have to say anything," Max said. "But I want to say thank you."

"What?" Lisa was startled. "Why?" She had been trying to figure out how to tell Max how sorry she was for what had happened. She was sure that he would be upset about it, maybe even angry that she had taken matters into her own hands.

"What you did was very brave, and very smart," Max said. "Most of all, it was very kind. You saw that Pepper was in a lot of pain, and you took responsibility for making the tough decision to end that pain for him. I'm just glad you had the guts to do it."

Lisa still didn't know what to say. She wanted to tell Max that she didn't deserve his thanks, because she almost hadn't had the courage to do what she had done. She had almost let her own selfish wish to keep Pepper with her forever get in the way.

Luckily, Max saved her from answering by turning to Carole and Stevie. "And I guess you two probably deserve some thanks, too," he said. "You three girls always help each other out. I'm sure Lisa was glad for your support."

"That's true," Lisa said, giving her friends a grateful smile.

"No problem," said Stevie. Lisa and Carole both noticed the devilish gleam in her eyes as she gave Max a sidelong glance. "Now, why don't you tell us about *your* weekend?"

"Oh, we will," Max said casually. "But first I want to hear more about what happened here while I was away."

Carole tried to hide a grin at Stevie's frustrated look. She knew that Stevie was hoping to get some news about Max's mystery woman. But she also knew that it was awfully hard to get Max to talk about anything before he was good and ready to do so.

"Well, there's not much to tell, really—" Stevie began.

Mrs. Reg interrupted her. "How's Samson doing?" she asked briskly. "Did you have a chance to continue his training while we were gone? You know how important it is to reinforce what he's already learned."

"I know," Stevie said. "I think Red did some work with him the other day, and I worked with him on the lunge line for a few minutes yesterday in the indoor ring."

"Where is Red, anyway?" Max asked, glancing around. "I'm going to need his help in a few minutes."

"I think he went out to get some lunch," Carole vol-

132

AUTUMN TRAIL

unteered. "The other stable hands aren't back yet, so he waited to go until we got here, and I don't think he's come back yet."

"Hmmm," Max said, stroking his chin. "Well, I suppose you girls can help me instead."

"Help with what?" Stevie asked, instantly curious.

"In a minute," Max said. "First, tell me how Barq is doing. Is that scratch on his flank healing all right?"

"You can hardly see it anymore," Stevie answered impatiently. "But, Max . . ."

"And what about Harry?" Mrs. Reg inquired. "He seemed to be getting a little bit of a cold before we left. . . ."

"All cleared up," Stevie said. "Judy checked him over and said he's fine."

"Good," Max said. "I hope you and Red exercised each horse at least once over the weekend. I know how worked up Garnet gets if she's cooped up for too long. Not to mention Geronimo—I hope you let him out in the paddock to let off some steam once in a while. And Diablo is always a little wild after a few days without a saddle on his back. . . ."

"Don't worry," Stevie said, gritting her teeth. "Red took most of the horses out at least once while you were gone, and we let the others out in the paddock during the afternoons when it wasn't too cold."

Carole and Lisa could hardly keep from laughing at their friend's frustration, even though they were almost

133

as curious as she was about Max's holiday. Finally, after a few more questions, Max seemed satisfied that things had gone smoothly in his absence.

"Good job, Stevie," he proclaimed at last. "It sounds as though I left things in good hands. I'll have to start going on vacation more often."

Stevie groaned. "Not *too* often, I hope," she said. "I don't want to have to work that hard again for a long time. I have blisters on top of blisters. And more blisters on top of those!"

Max laughed. "Well, I think you *and* your blisters will forgive me when you see what I've brought back with me," he said mysteriously.

"What?" asked Stevie, Carole, and Lisa in one voice.

Max and Mrs. Reg exchanged a glance. "Should we introduce them now?" Max asked his mother.

Mrs. Reg nodded. "I think now would be a perfect time," she said. "I just hope they hit it off."

"What? Who?" Stevie demanded eagerly, looking from one to the other. "Where is she?"

Lisa glanced at the car Max and Mrs. Reg had just exited. There was no one waiting inside it as far as she could see. Max had to be talking about his girlfriend, but where was she?

"Did you bring your girlfriend back with you?" Carole blurted out without thinking. As soon as the words were out of her mouth, her face turned bright red. "I—I . . . mean . . . I, " she stammered.

Max looked confused. "What are you talking about?"
Carole just shrugged, unable to speak.

Stevie, who was almost never at a loss for words, decided it was time to try the direct approach. "Isn't that what you were doing this weekend, Max?" she asked. "Visiting your girlfriend?" She smiled triumphantly, proud that The Saddle Club had figured out his secret.

But much to her surprise, Max burst out laughing. "Whatever gave you that idea?" he asked when he was able to stop laughing long enough to speak. Mrs. Reg was laughing, too.

"Well," Carole said uncertainly, "we thought that's what this trip was all about." She glanced at her friends, who were beginning to look almost as embarrassed as she felt. Feeling somewhat responsible for the whole situation, which suddenly seemed to be turning out to be some kind of huge misunderstanding, Carole tried to explain. "I sort of accidentally overheard you talking on the phone about a special lady named Lillian, so naturally we thought you were going to visit your girlfriend for a romantic weekend." She decided to leave out their speculations about his impending marriage and/or elopement.

"And why do you think I came along on this romantic weekend, then?" Mrs. Reg asked with a chuckle. "After all, Max is old enough not to need a chaperon."

"I guess we didn't really think about that," Stevie mumbled.

"Besides," Max said, "if you thought I was about to introduce you to a girlfriend, where did you think she was now? Did you think I made her ride in the trailer?" He gestured to the empty car.

"I guess we didn't think about that, either," Stevie admitted, her face flaming.

"Hey, Max, why did you bring the trailer with you, anyway?" Lisa asked curiously.

"Well, girls, I'm not even going to lecture you about listening to other people's phone conversations," Max said, ignoring Lisa's question. "*This* time," he added quickly, making it clear that he did not approve of their eavesdropping.

"So who did you want us to meet?" Stevie asked, partly to change the subject before Max changed his mind about that lecture, but mostly because Max still hadn't told them what he'd really been doing that weekend.

"Well, you were partly right when you thought I'd been spending the weekend with a very special lady," Max began. He started walking toward the horse trailer, and the girls followed eagerly.

"Oh, Max!" Carole exclaimed, catching on at last. "Did you buy another horse?"

Max smiled, and Carole knew she'd guessed correctly.

"Oh, Max, that's wonderful!" Stevie cried. "Is she in the van now?"

Max nodded. "As you know, ever since I got Geronimo, I've been looking for a new mare to breed with him. And I finally found her."

By this time they had reached the van, and Max carefully swung open the wide back door. The girls peered into the dark interior of the van, where they could see a tall, slender horse cross-tied in one of the two stalls.

"How wonderful," Carole said breathlessly. "Can we bring her out now so we can see her better?"

"Did you think I was going to leave her in there all day?" Max asked, trying—unsuccessfully—to sound gruff. Carole could tell that he was just as excited about the new addition to Pine Hollow as they were. "Carole, why don't you do the honors. But be careful. She's had a long ride."

Carole nodded. She knew that even the gentlest of horses could sometimes be upset by a long van ride. But she also knew that Max wouldn't let her bring the horse out if he wasn't fairly certain she wouldn't act up. He was just reminding her to be cautious, which was always a good reminder to have when working with horses.

She climbed into the van. Stevie and Lisa helped Max lower the ramp off the back as Carole approached the mare carefully from behind, talking reassuringly to her all the while. It was never good to surprise a horse by coming up to it suddenly from the rear, especially a strange horse who might be a kicker.

The mare's small, delicate ears flicked backward, and she turned her head as far as the lead ropes would allow.

Carole could see that the horse had the delicate, aristocratic head and the long, slender neck of a Thoroughbred. "You're a beauty," Carole whispered to the horse, reaching forward slowly to unhook the lead lines from the side of the van. "Now come on out with me so you can check out your new home. You're going to love it here." She knew that the horse couldn't understand what she was saying, but that the tone of her voice was what mattered. She tried to make it as soothing as possible so that the mare would know she didn't have anything to fear.

In a matter of moments, Carole had the mare out of the van. Both the girl and the horse blinked in the strong November sunlight. Carole handed the lead line to Max and then stepped back for a better look.

"Wow! What a great-looking horse," Stevie exclaimed, echoing Carole's thoughts.

The mare really was a beauty. She was tall for a mare, with a long, slender neck and an intelligent face. Her coat, which was a medium-chestnut shade, gleamed in the sun where it wasn't covered by the blanket strapped on her. She had four white socks and a little strip of white on her forehead that resembled a question mark. "What's her name?" Carole asked Max without taking her eyes off the mare.

"Well, her full registered name is Al's Calypso Lady," Max said, stroking the mare's velvety nose. "She started out as a racehorse. But I think around here we can just call her Calypso."

"Calypso," Carole repeated, trying the name out. She decided it fit the horse perfectly. While helping Judy Barker on her rounds, Carole had spent some time at a local racetrack, where she had learned a little bit about the sport of racing. In fact, she had been surprised to find out how much there was to know—it was almost like a whole new world. Since Carole was determined to learn as much as humanly possible about every subject having to do with horses, she had taken her own ignorance about racing as a challenge and checked out of the library a few books on the subject.

Among the things she had learned was that American Thoroughbred racehorses, who all had to be registered at birth with the American Jockey Club, sometimes had strange names because of the rules for registration. These rules stated that a horse's name couldn't have more than eighteen characters, including spaces and punctuation. The horse couldn't have the same name as any other registered horse that was still living, or had been dead fewer than fifteen years. And it couldn't have the same name as any of racing's greatest stars, such as Man O'War or Eclipse, no matter how long ago they had lived.

"Calypso is the perfect name for her," Stevie agreed. She stepped forward to pat the mare's nose and get acquainted. Calypso turned her large, liquid brown eyes toward Stevie, seeming to smile. Her delicate ears flicked forward alertly.

"She's so beautiful," Lisa said. "I mean, she's *really* beautiful!"

Carole laughed. "You're such a sucker for a pretty Thoroughbred face," she teased her friend.

Lisa laughed, too, mostly because she knew it was true. Next to Pepper, Lisa's favorite horse in the stable was a lovely bay Thoroughbred mare named Prancer. Like Calypso, Prancer also had started as a racehorse, but a weak bone in her foot had ended her racing career and made it possible for Max and Judy Barker to buy her.

"Lisa's right, though," Stevie said. "Calypso is a beauty, and she looks fast, too, and young. And she doesn't look injured or anything as far as I can tell. So how come she's not still racing?"

"I suppose that's your tactful way of asking how I could afford such a fantastic horse," Max said.

Stevie grinned. "Well, maybe," she admitted.

Luckily, Max didn't take offense. "You're right, she is an excellent horse, with amazing racing bloodlines. And I wouldn't have had a prayer of buying her, except for a lucky accident she had in her last race."

"What do you mean?" Lisa asked. She'd thought that any accident a horse had was *un*lucky. "Did the same thing happen to Calypso that happened to Prancer?"

"No, no, nothing like that," Max hurried to assure the girls. "No, believe me, Calypso doesn't have any hereditary weakness in her bloodlines—anything but. And she wasn't injured, not physically at least."

"What, then?" Stevie demanded. She was getting tired of Max's mysterious, roundabout way of explaining things today. "What's wrong with her?"

"Well, this is what happened," Max said. "Calypso here has some of the best bloodlines I've ever seen. Her first race was a maiden race, which means that none of the horses running in it had ever won a race before. She won it easily, even though she was running against colts as well as fillies."

Carole, Stevie, and Lisa knew from their experience with Prancer that colts were usually faster than fillies. In fact, there were separate races exclusively for fillies and mares, although they often raced against male horses as well. So the fact that Calypso had won her first race against colts made her victory even more impressive.

"Then what happened?" Carole asked.

"Then what happened was her second race," Max said. "Her owners were so pleased with her performance that they decided to run her against colts again. The jockey had told them that she hadn't even exerted herself to win the first time. He was convinced that there was nothing this horse couldn't do, and the owners agreed."

Looking at Calypso, The Saddle Club could believe that. "Did she win the second race, too?" Lisa asked expectantly.

"Not exactly," Max said. "She was in fine form on race day and was the favorite to win, but things went badly for poor Calypso from the start of the race. First she got boxed in behind several other horses. She just couldn't find a way around them, and she got frustrated. She wanted to be out front where she knew she belonged, I guess. But that wasn't the worst of it. About halfway through the race, one of the horses in front of Calypso stumbled and went down, taking a couple of other horses with him."

"Oh, no!" gasped Carole. It sounded a lot like what had happened to Prancer, although in that case she had been the only one to fall. Even though most races went off without incident, Carole knew that accidents did happen.

"Yes," Max said grimly. "It was a pretty bad accident from what I hear. Luckily for Calypso here, she managed to jump over the injured horses in front of her. But there was a lot of bumping going on both before and after the accident, and it must have spooked her pretty badly, because instead of finishing the race, she jumped the rail to the infield. Her jockey had a hard time staying in the saddle and keeping her under control—he was lucky he wasn't hurt. After that Calypso refused to stay on a track with more than one or two other horses. I guess she just didn't want to take a chance of going through the same kind of thing again. For more than a year, her trainer tried everything he could to cure her, but nothing helped. It was obvious she was useless as a racehorse."

"That's terrible," Carole declared. "Poor Calypso. She must have been so scared." She gave the horse, who looked anything but scared at the moment, a pat on the neck. "But if her bloodlines are as good as you say, wouldn't she be valuable as a brood mare?"

Max shrugged. "Maybe, but remember, she was practically untested on the track. Her time in that first race was fast enough to win, obviously, but it wasn't spectacular. Her jockey thought she could do a lot better, but people aren't willing to risk the big money involved on what a jockey thinks."

Carole knew that that was true. She had been surprised to discover what a big business Thoroughbred racing really was. "Still," she began carefully, "wouldn't the owner want to at least try? Before, I mean . . ." She tried to think of a way to phrase her question that wouldn't seem to be an insult to Max. After all, Pine Hollow was doing fine financially, but as far as Carole knew, Max wasn't exactly in a position to pay the tens of thousands of dollars that Calypso was probably worth whether she could race or not.

Suddenly Mrs. Reg started laughing. "Girls, Max isn't telling you the whole story," she said, her eyes twinkling.

"What do you mean?" Stevie asked, instantly sensing that something interesting was coming. She was even more certain about that when she noticed that Max was beginning to look embarrassed.

But before he could open his mouth to protest, Mrs. Reg was explaining exactly what she meant. "You see, one of these owners Max keeps referring to is a woman he went to high school with. Her name is Lillian Shepardson. You might say that she and Max were quite an item at the time."

"An old sweetheart?" Stevie exclaimed. "How romantic!"

"So we were partly right, after all," Carole said. "Max was going to see his old flame, maybe rekindle their love . . . ?"

"I don't think so," Mrs. Reg said drily. "This old flame has been married to someone else for many years and has five children. But she knows Max well enough to know he'll give Calypso a good home. So when it became clear they weren't going to get as much as they'd hoped for her anyway, she convinced the other owners to lower the price enough so that we could afford her—on the condition that they can breed her to one of their stallions someday and keep the foal." She smiled. "It's really a very generous deal from our point of view. *Very* generous." She gave the girls a wink. They realized that she was teasing Max by making it sound as if Lillian Shepardson had lowered the price only because she was still in love with him. Even though that probably wasn't true at all, The Saddle Club still thought it was awfully romantic that Max's high-school sweetheart had made it possible for him to buy such a beautiful horse.

"All right, girls," Max said suddenly, turning Calypso and starting to lead her in the direction of the stable. "We can't leave this fine Thoroughbred standing out in the cold all day, can we? Let's go. Since Red isn't back yet, you three will have to help get her settled in her new stall."

The Saddle Club exchanged glances. They could tell that Max was embarrassed by the story Mrs. Reg had told, and that he had decided to ignore it and pretend it had never happened. The girls smiled. Even though they all—even Stevie— knew better than to ever bring up the subject again, it was fun knowing something so personal about Max.

"Well, Calypso is *lovely*. I'm sure Geronimo will just *love* her," Stevie said. When Max turned to glare at her, she pasted an innocent smile on her face.

13

Once inside, Mrs. Reg said good-bye to the girls and headed for her office beside the tack room. Max led Calypso through the stable's entryway toward the U-shaped row of stalls. The Saddle Club was right behind him. "Where are you going to put her?" Carole asked.

"Well," Max said thoughtfully, "I was planning to put her in that empty stall next to Comanche's. But now I have a better idea." He paused for a moment and glanced past Calypso's nose at Lisa, who was walking on the mare's other side. "I'd like to put her in Pepper's stall."

Lisa didn't say anything at first. Carole and Stevie exchanged a worried glance. Even though their friend seemed to be handling Pepper's death quite well, they were afraid it was too soon for her to accept another

146

horse taking his stall. Carole, especially, remembered how difficult it had been for her to visit Cobalt's empty stall after he had died. She couldn't imagine how she would have felt if Max had moved another horse in there right away, but she was sure it would have been upsetting.

But Lisa's response was a big smile. "I think that's a wonderful idea," she told Max sincerely.

At that Carole was reminded once again that the three members of The Saddle Club were very different people. She couldn't always expect her friends to respond to things the same way she would. But she *could* count on them always to be her friends, and always to be horse crazy.

They proved the second point in the next few minutes as they got Calypso settled in her new home. Max handed Carole the mare's lead line in front of Pepper's stall and went off to check on the other horses, leaving the girls to be the official welcoming committee.

Apparently, Red had known Calypso was coming, because the stall, which Stevie had cleaned out thoroughly earlier that morning, had a layer of fresh clean straw on the floor. But there was still a lot to do. Carole removed Calypso's blanket, folded it, and headed off toward the tack room to put it away. Stevie took the clean water bucket from the stall and went to fill it. Meanwhile, Lisa started giving Calypso a good grooming. Her reddish mane was tangled after her long ride, and as Lisa gently worked through the knots with a wide-toothed comb, she talked to the mare.

"You know, Calypso," she began, "if you're going to be living in this stall, you've got a pretty big set of horse-shoes to fill. But I think if any horse deserves to be here, you just may be the one."

The mare nickered softly. Lisa wasn't sure if it was in response to her words or if Calypso was just enjoying being fussed over, as many horses did. She suspected it was the latter. But she continued to talk anyway, telling Calypso all about Pepper.

She was interrupted by her friends, who had returned from their separate errands. Stevie was lugging a full bucket of water in one hand and holding a flake of hay in the other.

"Get the door for me, will you?" she said breathlessly to Carole, who had just returned from the tack room.

Carole did better than that. After sliding open the stall door, she relieved Stevie of the heavy water bucket and hung it on its place while Stevie put the hay in the hayrack. The mare snuffled at the water, then at the hay. She took a few pieces of hay delicately in her mouth and munched at them slowly.

"She's deciding if the food's good enough to stay here," Stevie decided. Apparently it was, because Calypso took another mouthful when she'd finished the first.

Lisa smiled at the horse. "I was just telling her she's

got a lot to live up to, being in this stall," she told her friends.

"That's for sure," Carole said, leaning against the wall. "Pepper was one in a million. No, make that two million."

"Well, I for one am glad that Max decided to put Calypso in Pepper's stall," Stevie declared. She grinned. "After all, that means Veronica can't move Garnet in here."

"I'm glad, too, but not just for that reason, although it is a good one," Lisa said.

"Really? I was afraid you'd be upset," Carole admitted. "After all, Pepper has only been gone for a day, and already another horse is here in his place."

"I guess you could look at it that way," Lisa said thoughtfully. "But I think it's nice that Calypso is here. After all, someday soon she'll probably have a foal. Since she's staying in this stall, the foal will almost be part of Pepper, too." She paused, with the feeling that she wasn't explaining herself very well. "Do you know what I mean?"

Carole looked confused, but Stevie nodded. "I think I do," she said. "None of us will ever forget Pepper, but Calypso is proof that life goes on, and that's important. Putting her in here is almost a tribute to Pepper, in a way." She reached up and scratched the mare behind her ears. Calypso lowered her head and half closed her eyes in enjoyment. "Especially since she seems to be just as gentle and friendly as he was."

"Thanks," Lisa said to Stevie with a smile. "That's just exactly what I was trying to say."

Stevie blinked. "Does that mean I've finally learned to speak Lisa-ese?" she asked.

"I think it just means you're a really good friend," Lisa replied. She stopped grooming Calypso long enough to give Stevie a hug. "Thanks."

"What are friends for?" Stevie replied, hugging her back. Then she noticed that Carole was staring into space, looking distracted. She reached over and poked her. "Carole? What's on your mind?"

"Just what you said about Pepper's stall and everything. I never thought about it like that before," Carole said slowly. "I guess I see what you guys mean, but I still can't help thinking that there should be something else we can do to show how important Pepper was to us."

"I was thinking about that a lot last night," Lisa said, a bit shyly. "I had an idea."

"What?" Carole and Stevie asked in one voice.

"Well," Lisa began, hoping her friends wouldn't think she was silly, "just before Pepper—well, just before the end, I kept thinking there was something I wanted to say to him, you know, to sort of sum up everything he's been to me."

Carole and Stevie nodded, understanding perfectly.

"So," Lisa continued, "I finally realized that the only

thing I could think of was to thank him. For all the good times and everything, and for always being such a good friend to me and to everyone else."

Carole and Stevie nodded again. "What's your idea, then?" Carole asked.

"I want to ask Max if we can put up a plaque by Pepper's paddock. It could go on the fence, right there in the shade of that big oak tree where he used to stand when it got hot," Lisa said. "All it would need to say is his name, and 'thank you.' It could sort of be from everyone who ever knew him."

"What a wonderful idea," Carole whispered. Even though she and Lisa might have very different ways of looking at things sometimes, she knew that the most important thing was that they had both loved Pepper. So had Stevie, and most of the other riders at Pine Hollow. The plaque sounded like a perfect way to help keep his memory alive for all of them, and Carole was glad that Lisa had thought of it. "It's especially perfect considering that it's Thanksgiving time. Whenever we see the plaque, we'll always remember to be thankful for Pepper—and for all the other horses, too," she added, thinking of Starlight.

"Definitely," Stevie added. "It's absolutely perfect. Let's ask Max about it right away."

Carole cleared her throat. "Well, actually, if you don't mind too much, could we wait a couple of hours before we talk to Max?"

Lisa and Stevie both shrugged. "Sure," Lisa said. "I'm sure he'll be busy for a while getting settled in after his trip, anyway. But why? Are you still embarrassed about our mistake?" She grimaced at the memory. She could hardly believe that they had confused Max's plans to buy a new horse with a romantic rendezvous—although, as it turned out, there really had been more than one "special lady" involved if they counted Calypso *and* Lillian.

"No, it's not that," Carole said, a smile spreading across her face. "It's just that I realized we've all been breaking one of the cardinal rules of The Saddle Club."

"What do you mean?" Stevie demanded. "Just because you two weren't much help when I was mucking out stalls all week"—she gave a mock groan and grabbed her back, pretending to be in pain from all the work— "doesn't mean we weren't all helping each other out in other ways. . . ."

"No, no, that's not what I meant," Carole interrupted. By now the smile was a full-fledged grin. "I'm talking about the other rule, being horse crazy. I mean, think about it. We've been so busy with our various Saddle Club Thanksgiving projects that we haven't been riding in at least . . ."

"Four whole days," Stevie and Lisa finished the sentence for her, their eyes growing wide as they realized she was right.

"I think a trail ride is in order, pronto!" Carole said,

straightening up and giving her best Marine Corps salute.

"Aye, aye, sir," Stevie said, giving a rather sloppy salute in return. "Let's saddle up and hit the trail!"

"Sounds good to me," Lisa said. She gave Calypso's shiny coat a quick once-over with a cloth. Then, satisfied that the mare was comfortable, she and her two best friends gave her a good-bye pat, left Pepper's—now Calypso's—stall, and hurried off to tack up for their favorite activity. And they were all thankful for that.

ABOUT THE AUTHOR

BONNIE BRYANT is the author of more than fifty books for young readers, including novelizations of movie hits such as *Teenage Mutant Ninja Turtles®* and *Honey, I Blew Up the Kid*, written under her married name, B. B. Hiller.

Ms. Bryant began writing The Saddle Club in 1986. Although she had done some riding before that, she intensified her studies then and found herself learning right along with her characters Stevie, Carole, and Lisa. She claims that they are all much better riders than she is.

Ms. Bryant was born and raised in New York City. She lives in Greenwich Village with her two sons.